CHARLIE BUMPERS vs. THE END OF THE YEAR

Bill Harley

Illustrated by Adam Gustavson

PEACHTREE

ATLANTA

Published by
PEACHTREE PUBLISHING COMPANY INC.
1700 Chattahoochee Avenue
Atlanta, Georgia 30318-2112
www.peachtree-online.com

Edited by Vicky Holifield
Design by Nicola Simmonds Carmack
Composition by Adela Pons

The illustrations were rendered in India ink and watercolor.

Printed in January 2020 in the United States of America by LSC Communications in Harrisonburg, VA

10 9 8 7 6 5 4 3 2 1 (hardcover)
10 9 8 7 6 5 4 3 2 1 (trade paperback)

HC ISBN: 978-1-68263-042-6
PB ISBN: 978-1-68263-162-1

Library of Congress Cataloging-in-Publication Data

Names: Harley, Bill, 1954– author. | Gustavson, Adam, illustrator.
Title: Charlie Bumpers vs. the end of the year / Bill Harley ; illustrated by Adam Gustavson.
Other titles: Charlie Bumpers versus the end of the year
Description: First edition. | Atlanta : Peachtree Publishers, [2019] | Summary: Charlie springs into action when he learns that one of his best friends, Hector, who will move back to Chile at the end of fourth grade, is being bullied.
Identifiers: LCCN 2018038457 | ISBN 9781682630426
Subjects: | CYAC: Best friends—Fiction. | Friendship—Fiction. | Bullying—Fiction. | Schools—Fiction. | Behavior—Fiction. | Family life—Fiction. | Humorous stories.
Classification: LCC PZ7.H22655 Ce 2019 | DDC [Fic]—dc23 LC record available at *https://lccn.loc.gov/2018038457*

This book is dedicated, with gratitude, to
Vicky Holifield, editor extraordinaire and
Charlie's cheerleader

Special Thanks

Children who grow into strong people are those who are surrounded by a lot of caring people. In Charlie's case, he has been supported by a whole family of encouraging, intelligent readers. Without them, he would not have become who he is. And so, Charlie and I offer our deepest thanks to Jane Murphy, Amy Brittain, Debbie Block, Nicole Geiger, Kassie Randall, Michele Eaton, and especially Margaret Quinlin and all of Charlie's extended family at Peachtree Publishing Company Inc.

Contents

1

Fourth Grade Forever!

Before I knew it, the school year was almost over! It was May, and there were only a couple more weeks left. Everyone in my fourth-grade class was talking about what they were going to do that summer and who their teachers might be next year.

I must be crazy. I was going to miss fourth grade.

Don't get me wrong. I, Charlie Bumpers, am ALWAYS happy to get out of school. But looking ahead, I realized I was happy where I was.

I would never admit it to my parents or my brother Matt—or even to my teacher, Mrs. Burke—but I was going to miss my class. At the beginning of the year,

I didn't like Mrs. Burke, but now I really did. And I liked our class.

Except for Samantha Grunsky, who has driven me crazy all year long.

I especially liked Hector. His family moved here last fall from Santiago, Chile, and he ended up in my class, sitting right beside me. Since he was new, and English wasn't his best language, he was kind of shy and didn't have many friends. But I found out right away that he was a really nice guy, and also very good at soccer. Pretty soon we became friends. As the year went on, he got to know a lot of the kids in the school and everyone seemed to like him. Mostly he hung out with me and my other best friend, Tommy Kasten. We were even all on the same soccer team, and we would be next year, too.

But the reason I hated to see fourth grade end was I didn't know what would happen in fifth grade.

Things could change.

What if I got Mrs. Blumgarden, the teacher I

knocked over—by accident—in the hallway? And what if Hector wasn't in my class? Or Tommy?

Just Samantha Grunsky!

Disastrophe! (That's a disaster and a catastrophe together.)

And Matt told me that fifth grade is a lot harder than fourth grade. He said there's more homework and the teachers are tougher because they're getting you ready for middle school.

"They'll eat you alive in middle school!" Matt told me.

"Stop terrorizing your younger brother," Dad said.

That's what Dad always says.

But maybe Matt was right. Maybe fifth grade *would* be hard.

I liked things the way they were. Except for maybe getting to have Tommy in my class, I didn't want anything to change.

As far as I was concerned, I could stay in fourth grade forever.

I was thinking all those things when I sat down for dinner with my family. I wanted to talk about it when it was my turn to share, which we do every night. But before I could say anything, my little sister opened her mouth.

2

Just Say NO!

"I have news today," the Squid announced. "It's very important."

My little sister Mabel—I call her the Squid—is a first grader. Even though the school year was almost over, she still thought everything was important and new.

It wasn't new for me. I'm in fourth grade, so I've known all about first grade forever. Or at least since first grade, which makes three years.

My whole family was at our dining table—Mom, Dad, my older brother Matt, and the Squid. Dad had made a huge casserole with tons of cheese on top, which was very promising. I was starved.

"Can we eat a little first and then hear all about it?" Dad asked.

"You can eat while I talk," the Squid said. "But you have to listen while you eat."

She took a big helping of the casserole and stuffed a bite in her mouth. She chewed as fast as she could, swallowed, and took a gulp of milk.

"Today"—she started talking before anyone else had taken a bite—"we had the second day of our unit on bullying. First we sang our song. It goes like this."

"Oh no!" I moaned. "Not again!" I put my hands over my ears.

"Aaaah!" Matt groaned. He covered his face and muttered something we couldn't hear.

The Squid pushed out her chair, planted her feet on the floor, and launched into the song.

"When someone's being bullied," she sang out in a voice that sounded like a dying seagull, "you STAND UP! And just say NO!" She jumped up from her chair and shook her head from side to side. Then she took a deep breath, sat back down, and kept going.

"When someone's being bullied, you STAND UP! And just say NO!"

We had all heard the song before. Last night at dinner, the Squid explained about the first-grade unit on bullying, and then she sang the dumb song for us—*three times.*

It was horrible last night, and it was worse tonight. But the Squid didn't care. She just kept singing.

Dad had a cockeyed grin on his face, like he was enjoying the nightmare of her wailing.

"When someone's being bullied, you STAND UP! And just say NO!" the Squid screeched, jumping to her feet every time she sang STAND UP! and stomping the floor when she sang NO!

"Just say NO!" she went on. "Until you make the bully go!"

"Mabel," Mom said gently. "The song is nice, but what else did you do?"

"We learned a new verse." My sister paused to catch her breath, but I could tell she was getting ready to sing again.

"Can you just *tell* us about it?" Mom asked.

The Squid sat down. "Okay, but it's more fun to sing."

"Fun for *you*," Matt said. "Torture for us."

"Matt!" Dad gave my older brother a warning look. "Mabel, just tell us about it."

"Today we learned about how you can tell if someone's being bullied."

"Give us a break, Mabel," Matt muttered. "We know this already."

"First, if someone is being bullied," the Squid lectured in her six-year-old-know-it-all way, "they might start acting different. Like they don't want to talk about something. Or you might know someone's being bullied if they don't have their lunch money because maybe someone's taking it from them, or you might tell someone's being bullied if they pretend to be sick so they can stay home, or..."

The Squid kept blabbing, but I was still thinking about what she'd said about someone suddenly acting different.

I nearly choked on my casserole.

My stomach twisted up in an enormous knot.

It felt like I was in a dark, winding tunnel, far away from everybody at the table. I knew the Squid was still talking, but I couldn't hear her anymore.

I was thinking about Hector.

3

Emergency Mode!

I remembered something that had happened a couple of weeks ago at recess. I was looking for Hector to be on a team so we could challenge some fifth graders to a game of basketball. I looked all over the playground until I found him in "the Corner" with Jaden Craig, Darren Thompson, and Butler Bowen.

The Corner is a part of the playground that's mostly hidden from view. It's a little place where a wall juts out beside the doors from the playground to the school. Teachers are always going over there and telling kids to come out in the open where everyone can see them.

I had never seen Hector talk with Darren before.

I almost never talked with Darren. Or Jaden or Butler.

Mostly, I tried to avoid those guys. So when I saw them in the Corner, I couldn't figure out why Hector would hang around with them.

Darren's in fourth grade, too, but he's been bigger than me ever since I met him in first grade. Once, in second grade, he pulled my underwear out of my pants. He was always telling me I was dumb and punching me in the arm for no reason. After he tripped me during a relay race in third grade, I decided to stay away from him as much as I could.

Jaden, a fifth grader, was a lot taller than me or Darren. I didn't know Butler, but I knew he was in fifth grade.

I figured if he ever got the chance, he would pull my underwear out, too.

Darren, Jaden, and Butler were definitely three guys to stay away from.

That day during recess, when I asked Hector if he wanted to play basketball, Jaden told me they were just talking and Hector said he'd see me later.

It wasn't like Hector at all to say no to a game, but he seemed okay with it, so I found somebody else to play with us.

When I asked him about it later, he shrugged and said they were just asking him some questions about South America.

I should have seen right then that something was wrong. Those guys weren't the kind of kids who cared about South America.

After school that same day, my friend Tommy and I saw them get on their bus with Hector. They followed him down the aisle and sat behind him.

"That's weird," Tommy said. "Hector never hangs out with those guys."

And then, just yesterday Hector had asked me if he could borrow a dollar. He said he had lost his lunch money. Hector had never asked to borrow money. *I* was the one who always needed money or lost things. Not Hector.

I gave him a dollar.

◆ ◆ ◆

Were those guys bullying Hector? My throat closed up, and my ears were ringing. The Squid was still talking.

"Mrs. Diaz says that a lot of times it's the shy kids who are bullied, because they're easy to pick on."

"No problem for you," Matt said. "You're not shy."

"I know," the Squid agreed. "Mrs. Diaz says I'm the opposite of shy."

The Squid wasn't shy, but Hector was.

"Charlie?" Mom asked all of a sudden. "Are you all right?"

"What?" I said.

"You've just been sitting there staring into space," she said. "Is there something wrong?"

"Um…no." I wasn't positive Hector was being bullied. And even if I was, I wouldn't have said anything right then. I knew if I did, my parents might go into Emergency Mode.

"Emergency Mode" is Matt's term. It's what happens when Mom and Dad think something is really wrong with one of us, and all of a sudden they turn into a special army squad doing ten things at once. They start asking questions, lecturing, and making phone calls to other adults.

They went into Emergency Mode once when the principal called them and said that Matt had pulled the fire alarm at school. When that happened, it seemed like all of us, even our dog Ginger, had pulled the fire alarm. We *all* got lectures.

And they went into Emergency Mode the time I tried to jump down six stairs at once and hit the little table at the bottom of the stairs with my head. I had to go to the emergency room and get stitches.

We all got a lecture for that, especially Matt, since he was the judge of the Stair-Jumping Olympics and the Squid and I were the Olympians.

I really did *not* want my parents going into Emergency Mode about Hector. And besides, what if I was wrong about all this?

"Are you sure you're okay?" Mom asked.

"Yes," I said, swallowing hard. "I'm fine."

"Did Mabel say something that made you uncomfortable?"

Oh no, I thought, *the interrogation is beginning!*

"No," I said.

"You're not being bullied are you, Charlie?" Dad asked.

"No!" I said. "No one's bullying me. I'm fine. Really!"

"Charlie," the Squid said, "if you're being bullied, you need to tell an adult. You need to…STAND UP! And just—"

"I'm fine!" I interrupted. "There's nothing wrong with me! And stop singing that dumb song!"

"Touchy, touchy," Matt said.

"I like that song," the Squid said.

"I'm not being bullied," I promised.

It wasn't me I was worried about.

4

Don't Say Anything

"Hector, wait!" Our class had just gone out the door for recess.

"What is it, Charlie?" he asked.

"Um, I was wondering something. Are you, like, friends with Darren and Jaden and Butler now?"

Hector took in a deep breath, let it out, and looked away. "No, not really."

"I was just wondering, because I keep seeing you with them. What are you guys talking about?"

"Nothing."

Hector looked down at his shoes, then around the playground, then up at the sky. Anywhere but at me.

"Are they bothering you?"

"It's okay." He took off his glasses and started rubbing them with his shirttail.

Hector always cleans his glasses when he's nervous.

"What do they want?"

"Nothing."

"Are they picking on you or something?"

Hector shrugged and looked away again.

"Did you give them that dollar?"

"I'll pay you back," he said.

"I don't care about the dollar, Hector."

"It's all right now. Just don't tell anyone, okay?"

"But Hector—"

"I can take care of things," he said. "I have to do it myself. And Charlie, *please* don't tell anyone."

"Maybe we can figure out how to make them stop," I said. "Or maybe you could tell someone—"

"No!" Hector said. "I don't want to do that. If those guys found out, it would just make them madder. And my father says when I have a problem, I have to take care of it myself. He says I shouldn't be *un soplón.*"

"A what?"

"My dad says someone who tells on others is a *soplón.*"

"Like a tattletale?"

"I guess so. Anyway, I really don't want anyone to call my parents."

"Yeah, but if you don't do something, then they're just going to keep bugging you."

"I know," Hector said, "but it doesn't really make any difference. School's almost over anyway."

"Yeah," I said. "But what about next year?"

Hector shook his head. "Not a problem."

"Why not? They'll just keep bugging you in fifth grade."

"No, they won't. I won't be here."

"What do you mean? Where will you be?"

"When school is over, we're moving back to Santiago."

"What? Why?"

I couldn't believe it! Hector couldn't move back to Chile! He was one of my best friends!

"My dad's company wants him to come back. My parents told me last week. I wanted to tell you, but I haven't had a chance."

I was flabbergasted. "Are you sure you have to move back? Couldn't your parents stay just one more year?"

"I don't think so."

"But you and your mom could stay. She could

work here! You can't leave—you're just getting to know everything. And next year our soccer team is going to be really good. And maybe you and me and Tommy will all be in the same class. We'll be fifth graders—like kings of the school!"

"I know," he said.

"You *have* to stay."

"I wish I could." Hector looked miserable.

Hector leaving was as bad as Jaden and Darren and Butler bullying him. Now I really, *really* didn't want fourth grade to end. I wanted the end of the school year to go away.

We stood there, looking out at all the other kids running around on the playground. Over by the wall of the gym, I saw Darren, Jaden, and Butler pushing each other around and laughing. Hector saw them, too.

"Those guys are bozos," I said. "I wish we could do something about them."

"I guess the good thing is they won't be able to bother me. I'll be too far away."

"Right," I said. "But they'll still be bozos."

"Complete bozos," Hector said. Then he smiled. Hector had this great smile that spread all the way across his face and made his eyes crinkle up. I realized that I hadn't seen it for a while. I wondered how long those guys had been giving him a hard time.

Why hadn't I noticed?

The teachers blew the whistles for the end of recess, so Hector and I had to go back inside.

"Don't say anything," Hector said to me again. "Please."

"Okay," I said. But it didn't feel right.

5

The Jerzollies
of Darkness

"I don't believe it," Tommy said. "Hector can't move away! We can't let the Strikers win the soccer league again. We, the almighty Pirates, will be bigger and faster and better next year. Especially with Hector."

"I know," I said.

Tommy had come over after school, and we were in my bedroom. He was lying on his back on the floor with his legs up on my bed. I was sitting on the floor leaning up against the door of my closet, which wouldn't close all the way because of all the stuff in it.

"Hey, by the way," Tommy said, "I saw those guys, Darren and Jaden and Butler, following Hector down the hall just after school let out. Do you think they're bullying him or something?"

"Um, maybe." I remembered what Hector said about not telling anyone.

"They are, aren't they?" Tommy asked. He could tell I knew something. "You have to tell me."

"Um, sort of," I admitted.

"I knew it," Tommy said. "Those guys are complete jerks."

"Jerks *and* bozos," I said.

"Right," Tommy said. "Jerky bozos."

"Bozoey jerks."

"Jerzos," Tommy said.

"Yes, jerzos. But bullies, too."

"Jerzollies!" Tommy announced.

"That sounds like some kind of sweet roll," I said.

"It is," Tommy explained. "It's a jerk and a bozo and a bully, all *rolled* into one. Put in the oven and baked at a thousand degrees until well done."

"Jerzollies!" We both laughed.

"The Jerzollies of Darkness!" Tommy crowed.

I jumped up and stood on my bed, raising my arms. "We will defeat the Jerzollies of Darkness!"

Tommy and I couldn't stop laughing. He climbed up on the bed with me.

"Defeat the Jerzollies of Darkness! Defeat the Jerzollies of Darkness!" we chanted, leaping up and down on the bed.

"We are the Heroes of Vengeance!" Tommy screamed, flexing the muscles on his skinny arms.

That did it. I buckled over laughing. Tommy kept jumping, which made me laugh harder. My sides hurt.

Mom came in my room and just stood there. She didn't say anything. She didn't have to.

Tommy stopped jumping. "Hi, Mrs. Bumpers," he said, gasping for breath.

It took a few seconds for us to stop laughing.

"Tommy, do you have a rule in your house about jumping on beds?" Mom asked.

Trick question. No good answer.

"Um, yes," Tommy said.

"Well, so do we," Mom said as she went out the door. We listened to her footsteps going down the stairs.

We sat back down on the floor.

"So, we have two problems," Tommy said. "Hector moving, and the Jerzollies of Darkness.

Let's think about Hector moving first. We need a plan. A way to get him to stay."

"Maybe he could live at your house," I said. "Or at mine."

"Our house isn't very big. Unless he wants to sleep in the basement. Or on my floor."

"I doubt that he would stay with either of us," I admitted. "Besides, I don't think his parents would just leave him behind."

"Right. We have to think of something so important that his whole family would have to stay."

"Like what?" I asked.

"Well, like what if he had a really important job to do at school?"

"Something *super* important," I added.

"Stupifically important. Like the most important job in the school. Like principal. Except kids can't be principals."

Suddenly I leapt up off the floor and started jumping on the bed again.

"What is it?" Tommy climbed up and started jumping around, too.

"What's the most important job a kid at school can have? And a job that only fifth graders can have?"

"I...don't...know," Tommy said in between bounces. "Filling up...the dumpster? Sometimes... Mr. Turchin lets...fifth graders...fill up the dumpster."

"No! Not that! School Ambassador!"

Tommy's mouth opened wide and so did his eyes. "Stupific!" he shouted.

We started high-fiving each other every time we jumped up, then Tommy tackled me and we both fell off the bed.

Mom opened the door and looked down at us.

"Tell me you weren't jumping on the bed," she said.

"We weren't jumping on the bed," I said.

She gave us the evil-mom stare and closed the door on us. If she caught us jumping on the bed one more time, I might be banished from my own bedroom. But I was too busy thinking about my brilliant idea to worry about that.

At the end of every year, the fourth-grade teachers choose two students—a boy and a girl—to be the School Ambassadors for the coming year. The Ambassadors greet important people when they visit and give them school tours.

The Ambassadors were two of the most important people in the school.

If Hector was chosen as a School Ambassador, the school would need Hector for the whole year. Then maybe his parents would realize they had to stay.

And maybe Tommy would be in my class. And maybe Samantha Grunsky wouldn't. And maybe fifth grade wouldn't be so bad.

"Wait!" I said. "That might also solve our other problem. If Hector is a School Ambassador, there's no way those Jerzollies of Darkness are going to bug him anymore. No one ever bothers a School Ambassador!"

"He would be untouchable!" Tommy said. "A true Hero of Vengeance!"

"We are all Heroes of Vengeance!" I shouted.

"Now," Tommy said, "we just have to figure out how to get the teachers to choose him."

And that's how the Hector for School Ambassador Campaign started.

6

The Secret of Advertising

After Tommy left, I knocked on Matt's door. I wanted to tell him about our plan and ask his advice.

He didn't answer, so I figured he had his headphones on. Matt's always listening to music or making videos, since he's convinced he'll be the greatest movie maker in the world when he grows up.

I knocked harder.

"Go away!" he yelled.

I opened the door a crack. "Hey, Matt." I said, loud enough for him to hear.

"I told you to go away! What do you want?" He slid his headphones off one ear and turned around.

"I wanted to tell you something about Hector. It's really important."

He just looked at me.

"Hector's parents told him they're all moving back to Chile," I said.

"Bummer," Matt said. Then he started to put his headphones back on.

"Wait! So…Tommy and I don't want him to. For one thing, we need him on our soccer team next year. And besides, he's our best friend."

"What am I supposed to do about it?"

"Nothing. That's what I wanted to talk to you about. Tommy and I figured out a way to stop it."

Matt took his headphones off and let them hang around his neck. "How are you going to do that? You'd have to convince his parents, and convincing parents of something like that would be impossible."

"But if Hector was chosen to be School Ambassador, then his family would have to stay here."

"That's ridiculous," Matt said.

"How come?" I hated it when Matt told me my ideas were ridiculous.

"First of all, Charlie, just about the worst thing that can happen to anybody is to be named School Ambassador."

"What's wrong with it?"

"Charlie, it's a horrible job!"

"What do you mean? It's really important and you get out of class to meet people and everything."

"Big deal!" Matt said. "I'm telling you, Charlie, it's the Kiss of Death!"

"Huh?" I'd never heard of the Kiss of Death before.

"Think about it, Charlie. You have to be really good all the time! People are always watching you."

I knew about that. I'd had to be the Nice Gnome in the class play, and I hated my role. But Hector was different. "So? Hector *is* good all the time."

"No one wants to be good *all* the time. The Ambassador has to follow all the rules and set a good example for all the kids in the school."

"Hector would be good at that," I said. "He's always careful about following the rules."

"And every time you get in even a little bit of trouble, the teachers always remind you that you're different from everyone else and you have to try even harder."

"But Hector's a good example without even thinking about it! It's the perfect job for him."

"And kids are always teasing you about being the School Ambassador."

Hector was already being teased by Jaden and Darren and Butler—I didn't think it could get much worse.

"*I* wouldn't tease him," I said. "Neither would Tommy."

"He'd hate that job," Matt said. "Trust me."

I usually did trust Matt. Even when I shouldn't. But not this time.

"Maybe *I* would hate it," I argued, "but I'm not talking about me. I'm talking about Hector, and everything you say makes me think he's perfect for the job. And if it means he stays, then it's all worth it."

"Okay, but don't blame me if you curse him for life. Like I said, it's the Kiss of Death."

"I'll take that chance," I said. "But how do I get him to be chosen as School Ambassador?"

"I don't know, Charlie," Matt said. He was getting really exasperated. "I guess you have to promote him to the teachers."

"What do you mean, 'promote'?"

"Promotion is advertising, just like those dumb ads on television that keep saying the same thing over and over again. The first time you see one, you think it's ridiculous. But they keep playing it over and over again, and pretty soon you're believing them whether you want to or not. That's the secret of advertising. If you say it enough, people believe it."

"That's why they show those commercials over and over again?" I'd never thought about that.

"Yes!" Matt said. "You can convince anybody of anything if you just keep saying it enough times in different ways. Even if it's not true."

"But it *is* true. Hector would make a great School Ambassador."

"It doesn't make any difference if it's true or not. You just have to say it a thousand times."

"That's a lot," I said. "Will it even work on Mrs. Burke?"

"It works on anyone," he said. Then he put his headphones on, turned back to his computer, and pretended I wasn't there. I might as well have disappeared into thin air.

He had done such a good job explaining what I should do about promoting Hector for School

Ambassador, I wondered if I could ask him about Hector being bullied.

"Matt!" I called, loud enough for him to hear.

"OUT!" he yelled, pointing at the door without looking at me.

So I left.

I'd ask him about bullies later.

Matt was probably right about one thing—I would hate being School Ambassador. Luckily, there was no chance of that. Last year I accidentally hit Mrs. Burke in the head with a sneaker, and just this year I had knocked a fifth-grade teacher over in the hallway. Who would choose someone like that for Ambassador?

But the more I thought about it, the more it seemed like the perfect job for Hector. It might keep him from moving back to Chile.

And it might even solve the problem of the Jerzollies of Darkness.

Forget the Kiss of Death. It was time to use the Secret of Advertising.

7

One Down, Nine Hundred and Ninety-Nine to Go

On the bus, I told Tommy about the Secret of Advertising. "You just keep repeating your message until everyone believes it," I explained.

"Wow, that's amazing," Tommy said. "But I'm not sure it would work with my mom. If I keep asking for something, she usually tells me to put a sock in it."

"You have to say it a lot."

"How many times?"

"Matt says a thousand."

"A thousand times? Are you kidding?"

"I know. It's crazy. But we have to do it. Hector's life is at stake."

"Okay," Tommy said. "I'm in. But a thousand is a lot."

Before we got to school, we wrote out a list of steps to get Hector chosen.

Hector for Ambassador Campaign

1. Tell Mrs. Burke, Mrs. L, and Ms. Lewis that Hector would make a great Ambassador. At least a hundred times each.

2. Talk to other teachers about how great Hector is.

3. Tell the principal, Mrs. Rotelli, that Hector would make a great Ambassador.

4. Leave notes and posters around the school about how great Hector is.

5. Ask other kids to tell their teachers to vote for Hector.

Tommy and I agreed that our first job was to convince our own teachers that Hector should be Ambassador. We figured if Mrs. L (Tommy's teacher) and Mrs. Burke wanted Hector, he would have a great chance. We weren't sure how they made the decision, but having two fourth-grade teachers out of three on your side had to be good. Maybe Mrs. Burke's vote would count for more since she had been named Teacher of the Year last year.

Later that morning, I got my first chance to try out the Secret of Advertising.

Mrs. Burke finished a chapter from the book she was reading us, then said, "Now, Citizens of Mrs. Burke's Empire, I need some help."

Mrs. Burke called her class her "empire," and we were all her "citizens." She was kind of being funny, but also kind of being serious.

"Sarah, my Master Messenger, is out today," she said. "I need someone dependable to take all the books back to Mrs. Lefkowitz in the library. I'd like someone to collect them, count them, and pack them up." She pointed to a box on her desk.

A bunch of kids raised their hands. Everyone was eager to get out of class. Samantha Grunsky, the MOST ANNOYING PERSON ON THE PLANET (believe me), was behind me waving her arm and groaning like her appendix was bursting.

I raised my hand.

Okay, I waved it and groaned a little, too. "Oooh, oooh, oooh."

But I wasn't as annoying as Samantha Grunsky.

"Charlie," Mrs. Burke said, "do you think you can handle it?"

She asked me that because the last time I was Master Messenger I had knocked over Mrs. Blumgarden while I was flying down the halls pretending to be Buck Meson, the world's greatest superhero.

"No," I said.

Mrs. Burke frowned and her eyes scrunched

up—she looked at me like I was Buck Meson's loyal pet Crog, the three-headed alien creature from the planet Bronador.

"Are you saying you can't be trusted?" she asked.

"No…I mean, yes, I can. But I think Hector should do it. He's the most dependable person I know, and he would be good at collecting all the books and counting them. And making sure that Mrs. Lefkowitz gets them back. Hector would probably even help her put them on the shelves."

The class got quiet. Then *everyone* stared at me like I was Crog, the three-headed alien creature from the planet Bronador.

Even Hector. Who had not raised his hand.

"That's nice of you to say those things about Hector and volunteer him for a job," Mrs. Burke said. "But if he wants to do it, he can volunteer for himself."

Everyone looked at Hector to see if he would volunteer.

Hector looked embarrassed and shrugged his shoulders. "It's okay," he said. "Someone else can do it."

Mrs. Burke chose Dashawn Tremont to collect the books.

"That was really weird," Samantha Grunsky hissed at me. "Since when do you NOT want to get out of class?"

I ignored her. It *was* weird, but it was worth it. I had planted the idea in Mrs. Burke's brain that Hector was responsible and would make a great Ambassador.

One mention down, nine hundred and ninety-nine to go.

When we lined up for lunch, Hector asked me why I had volunteered him in class.

I smiled and patted him on the shoulder. "Don't worry, Hector. Tommy and I have a plan."

"What kind of plan?"

"A plan to solve all your problems," I promised.

I got one more chance to advertise to Mrs. Burke that afternoon. During silent reading time, she called us up one by one to her desk to talk about our personal essays.

When it was my turn, Mrs. Burke showed me some mistakes I had made.

"Keep working, Charlie," she said. "You just need to pay a little more attention."

I nodded.

"Any questions?" She looked down at her list to see who she would talk to next.

"Yes," I said.

"What is it?"

"Mrs. Burke, I was wondering about being School Ambassador," I said.

"Well, Charlie, that's something just the teachers and Mrs. Rotelli talk about and decide upon. Why? Is it something you'd like to do?"

"No. I mean, I'd like to, but I don't think I'd make a good School Ambassador."

"No?" She seemed kind of surprised when I said that.

"Well…you know," I muttered. I didn't want to remind her that I'd hit her in the head with a sneaker. How could she forget that?

She leaned back in her chair and folded her arms across her chest. "Why all the interest in Ambassadors all of a sudden?"

"Because I think Hector would be really good as School Ambassador next year. Probably the best ever."

"Thanks, Charlie," she said. "That's nice of you to say so. I'll keep your recommendation in mind."

"Okay." I said, and smiled.

"Is there anything else?"

"Um…I guess not, except that Hector would be a great Ambassador."

"Alright, then go back to your reading."

It didn't seem like Mrs. Burke had really paid much attention to me. But I remembered what Matt said about advertising. You just keep repeating your message over and over again. A thousand times. And I had just told her two more times.

Nine hundred and ninety-seven to go.

Right after school that afternoon, I reported my success at advertising to Tommy.

"I did some, too," he said. "I told Mrs. L. how great Hector is three times. Once when she came by my desk, once while we were standing in line waiting to get into the library, and once when she asked the class for an example of someone who had been a really good leader and stood up for something they believed in."

"Really?"

"Yeah, I think she was hoping someone would say Martin Luther King Jr."

"Well, we just have to keep doing it," I said. "And we need to talk to Mrs. Rotelli."

"We'd better do it together. And we'd better have a lot of reasons. Like five each. The principal is crucial in our campaign.

"Okay," I agreed. "Five each. That will make ten times we say it, which means we only have to say it nine hundred and eighty-four more times."

"We're almost halfway there!"

"No, we're not!"

"I know," Tommy said.

8

A Big Ball of
Tangled-Up String

The next day, while our class was finishing a
math assignment, Hector asked permission to go to
the restroom. He's always done with his work early.

Most of us had finished our assignment when
Mrs. Burke said, "Charlie, will you go see what's
keeping Hector?"

"Sure." I scooted out of my desk. As soon as I
got out of Mrs. Burke's sight, I hurried down the
hallway. I didn't fly like Buck Meson with rockets on
his shoes. I just jogged.

I pushed open the door to the boys' room. Hector was standing against the back wall.

In front of him was Jaden, with his back to me.

Hector was holding his glasses in one hand. He looked really nervous.

Jaden glanced back over his shoulder at me. "Hey," he said. "What do you want?"

Jaden took a step closer to me. I saw Hector shake his head at me, like I should just get out. My scalp started tingling. Even my hair felt tingly. "Um...I came down to see where Hector was," I said.

"He's right here," Jaden said. "He had to use the restroom. And so did I. So we were just talking. That's okay with you, isn't it?"

Now Jaden was standing right next to me, smiling like we were friends.

"Sure," I said. Maybe he was going to be nice after all.

"Good. I know you and Hector are friends. Even though he's from someplace else."

"Right," I said.

"Where is it you're from?" Jaden asked, turning back to Hector. "I forget."

Hector didn't say anything.

Jaden turned back to me.

When I first came in, I was worried about Hector. Now I was worried about both of us.

"Uh...he's from Chile," I said.

"Oh, right, Chee-lay!" Jaden said, making it sound weird. He rolled his eyes like it was a dumb place to be from. "Wherever that is, right?"

"Uh-huh," I said. I knew where it was. So did Jaden, I figured. Jaden was like Darren—sometimes I couldn't tell if he was joking around or being serious. It felt like if I said the wrong thing in the wrong way, he might get really mad.

"Um...Mrs. Burke wants Hector to come back to the classroom," I said.

"He'll be there in a minute," Jaden said. "He's washing his hands."

Hector wasn't washing his hands. He was just standing there.

"Go back and tell her that," Jaden said, taking

a step closer to me and looking down at my face. "Don't tell her anything else, though, okay, Charlie?"

What would Buck Meson my favorite superhero do?

Fix Jaden with an electron stare, freeze him on the spot, and yell, "I DON'T THINK SO!"

But when Jaden stared at me like that, I just wanted to get out of there. He was a big kid, and I didn't know what he would do.

I just nodded.

He pushed open the door, shoved me out in the hallway, and let the door swing shut.

I stood in the hall, my heart beating like crazy. I wanted to go back inside and get Hector. I wanted to tell Mrs. Burke about Jaden. I wanted to get Tommy and see what he would say. I even wished Matt was still in school here so I could tell him.

But instead, I just stood outside the door for a minute, wondering what to do. Finally, the door opened, and there was Hector, with Jaden right behind him.

"Why are you still here?" Jaden asked.

"Just waiting for Hector," I said.

"Well, here he is," Jaden said, giving Hector a push. "You'd better hurry up, so you don't get in trouble with your teacher."

Hector and I walked back to class without

talking. I wanted to tell him I was sorry, or that I should have been a better friend, or even that I was just too afraid to stand up to Jaden, but everything was jumbled together inside me like a big ball of tangled-up string.

Mrs. Burke didn't even notice when we got back. I was relieved.

Except for the little part of me that wished she *had* noticed.

I didn't want to tell, but I wanted her to find out.

When we were back in our seats, I snuck a look at Hector. He was rearranging things in his desk, which he didn't need to do.

"It's all right," he said, looking up at me. "Don't say anything. It'll just make things worse. And I can handle it. Really."

"Okay," I said.

And I didn't say anything.

Because he said it was okay. And because I was afraid.

9
It's Not That Easy!

Tommy had a doctor's appointment that after-noon so he wasn't on the bus. I stared out the window on the way home, thinking about Hector. As we walked to our house from the bus stop, the Squid babbled on and on, but I didn't even hear what she said.

Mom and Dad were both gone. Matt was upstairs in his room on his computer. The Squid and I had a snack of peanut butter and crackers and then I went outside.

I started kicking my soccer ball against the garage door. Our dog Ginger kept chasing after the ball, so

I kicked it harder and faster to try and keep it away from her.

The Squid stuck her head out the back door. "You're not supposed to do that," she said.

"I know," I muttered. I kept kicking the ball.

"You'd better stop now," she said. "I don't want to have to tell Mom and be a tattletale."

You mean a soplón, I thought.

As it turned out, the Squid didn't have to tell Mom, because Dad got home while I was still kicking the ball. He pulled the car really far up in the driveway and sat there glaring at me through the windshield.

I caught the ball, put it under my arm, and went inside without saying anything. Upstairs in my room, I tossed the ball in the corner and lay back on my bed, staring at the ceiling.

I was thinking that maybe Hector didn't even want to stay here, where bullies were picking on him and his friends weren't helping him. I wondered if there were bullies in Chile. There probably were—I figured bullies were found worldwide, like a disgusting mutant life form that had spread across the planet.

I heard Mom get home. In a little while she called me down for dinner.

Guess what the Squid talked about?

"Today we practiced what to do when someone is bullying you," she said. "The first thing you should do is tell them to stop. Then when they stop, you tell them how it feels so they understand, and…"

The Squid kept talking, but I stopped listening.

The way she talked, telling a bully to stop was the easiest thing in the world to do. To her it was no harder than saying, "Could I please have a glass of orange juice?" or "Would you please open the door?" But I knew that talking to bullies wasn't that easy.

"And then you should tell a grown-up so they know!" she went on.

That wasn't easy either. What if your best friend didn't want you to tell anyone?

"And then you should let the person who's being bullied know that you're their friend."

I couldn't take it anymore.

"IT'S NOT THAT EASY!" I shouted.

It got quiet. My whole family looked at me like there was something seriously wrong with me.

Today it seemed like everyone in the whole world was looking at me like I was Crog, the three-headed alien creature from the planet Bronador.

"Yes it is!" said the Squid, leaping up from her chair. "Don't you remember?"

Then she started in on that stupid song again.

57

"Stand up!" she sang. "And just say NO! JUST SAY NO! Until you make the bully GO!"

Then she sat down.

I just slumped in my chair and stared at the table. I wanted to paralyze my little sister with an electron stare.

It was ridiculously quiet. For about ten seconds.

"Why is it so quiet?" the Squid asked.

"Charlie," my mom said very softly. "Is there something wrong?"

I looked up at Matt. He raised his eyebrows to warn me.

Uh-oh. Emergency Mode.

First there would be a million questions. And then there would be phone calls. And Mom and Dad would whisper to each other. And Hector would never trust me again.

"No," I said.

"Are you sure?" she asked.

"Yes, I'm sure," I said. "I just don't think it's as easy as what Mabel says."

"I don't either," Dad agreed.

"It's not?" the Squid asked. "I'm just telling you what Mrs. Diaz said."

We finished dinner and no one talked very much. Not even the Squid, which was a minor miracle.

It was my turn to help clean up the dishes. So after dinner, it was just me and Mom in the kitchen.

I was hoping Emergency Mode was over.

But it wasn't.

"Charlie," Mom said. "It seems to me like there's really something bothering you. I think you need to tell me what it is."

Now I was really confused. Hector had told me not to tell, and there were a lot of reasons not to. But I needed to say something. So I told her part of it.

"I just found out that Hector's leaving. He's going back to Chile."

"Oh, honey, I'm sorry." She put her arm around

my shoulder and gave me a hug. "When are they leaving?"

"After school's out," I said. Now that I thought about it, Hector's leaving *was* really bothering me. A lot. I could feel my eyes filling up with tears. I didn't want Hector to go.

"He's a very good friend, isn't he?" she asked.

Okay. Now I was crying. I stuck my head in her armpit so she couldn't see. Unfortunately she knew. She rubbed my head.

Boogers.

That made me cry more.

"Why does he have to go?" I asked.

She didn't say anything. Maybe because it's a trick question, and there's no good answer.

She just hugged me some more, and I finally wiped the snot off my nose. Mom took a clean dish towel and dampened it and wiped off my face. We finished cleaning up.

I felt a little better. But I still hadn't found a way to deal with Jaden and Darren and Butler.

Those jerky bozo bullies. Those despicable Jerzollies of Darkness.

Where were the real Heroes of Vengeance when you needed them?

On one hand, I didn't want the school year to end, since Hector would leave. On the other hand, it couldn't end soon enough.

10
HECTOR ADÉLIA ROCKS!

Tommy got on the bus and bounced down the aisle, landing with a thud on the seat next to me. I wanted to tell him about what happened yesterday in the restroom, but I didn't get a chance.

"Look at this!" He unzipped his backpack and pulled out a big stack of papers. "My dad has a huge new copier at home because of a work project. He's only got it for a couple of weeks, but he let me use it last night. Campaign flyers!"

He held up a sheet of paper. On one side were these words in huge print:

HECTOR ADÉLIA ROCKS!

And underneath it, in smaller type:

Presented by the Hector

for School Ambassador Campaign

"Oh my gosh," I said. "This is stupific! You did this yourself?" It was so great I forgot all about the restroom catastrophe and Jaden the Jerzolly. "What do we do with them?"

"I've been thinking about that," Tommy said. "First, what about putting one up on the door of the teachers' room? That way every teacher would see it."

"That's a good idea. On the inside or outside?"

"Why not both? That way they see it twice—going in and coming out!"

"Awesome!" I said. Now I was getting pretty excited. "But we'll need lots of tape."

An evil smile spread across Tommy's face. He reached in his jacket pocket and pulled out a big roll of duct tape. "Ta da!" he said.

"Stupific!" I said.

"The trick is to make sure no one sees us putting

them up. We don't want people to know we're the ones behind the campaign."

"Exactly," I said. "Let's do it as soon as we get to school. Maybe no teachers will be in there then."

Tommy stuffed the roll of tape and the stack of flyers back into his backpack.

When we got off the bus, we headed inside and walked toward the teachers' room. Just before we got there, Tommy stopped and unzipped his backpack. "You hold the flyers," he said, "and I'll get some tape ready." He handed me a couple of sheets, then tore off two really long strips of tape and stuck them on his jacket.

"What if someone sees us?" I asked.

"We'll just say we're looking for our teachers."

"What if it *is* one of our teachers?"

"I don't know. We'll say we're looking for Mrs. Finch." Mrs. Finch was the school secretary.

Tommy opened the door and we peeked in. There was no one there. Without a word, we slipped inside.

"Quick," I said, holding one of the flyers against the door. "Give me some tape."

When Tommy tried to rip a piece of the tape off his jacket, some of it wrapped around his fingers. He tried to take it off, but it got more stuck and twisted.

"Hurry up!" I started to laugh. I was nervous.

"I'm trying! Can you pull it off my fingers? It's really sticky!" Now he was laughing, too.

I pulled the tape off his fingers, but then it got stuck on mine. When I finally got it off, it was wadded into a ball. "Give me some more tape," I said.

Tommy pulled the other strip off his jacket and I used it to stick the paper on the door as high as I could reach. I wanted to put another piece of tape on the bottom, but before I could, someone started to open the door. Tommy and I jumped back.

It was Mrs. Diaz, the Squid's teacher.

She frowned. "What are you boys doing here?"

"Um…just looking for our teachers," Tommy said.

"Mrs. Burke," I explained.

"And Mrs. L," Tommy added.

"Don't you think they're in their rooms, where *you're* supposed to be?"

Tommy looked around like he was trying to find a way to escape.

"I guess so, Mrs. Diaz," I answered. "We just got to school and haven't looked there yet."

"Fine," she said. "Why don't you go look there now?"

"Okay," Tommy and I said together. She opened the door for us, and we walked out. I didn't even look at Tommy, I just headed down the hall to class.

"Wait!" Tommy said in a loud whisper. "Give me the other sheet."

I handed it to him and looked around. "Hurry up before someone sees us!"

He took out the roll of duct tape and ripped off a huge strip, then stuck the flyer on the outside of the teachers' room door. It hung at an odd angle, but it didn't fall off.

"There," Tommy said. "Now they'll all be sure to see it."

We hurried down the hallway and turned onto the wing for fourth and fifth grade. I stopped to catch my breath. "Man, that was close," I said. "But we did it!"

"How many of the thousand times have we done now?"

"Not enough," I said. "But we're getting there."

I wasn't sure about where to put the rest of the flyers, but Tommy said he had an idea. He told me to meet him at the door of the cafeteria at lunchtime.

We high-fived and headed to our classrooms. The Heroes of Vengeance were now Masters of the Secret of Advertising.

11

Fast Is My Middle Name

"Let's go." Tommy headed down the hallway, and I hurried to catch up with him. The halls were empty. Kids were either in class or already in the cafeteria or on the playground.

"What are we doing?" I asked.

"Step Two in the Hector for Ambassador campaign. You know how the teachers all have little cubbyholes in the office where people put messages for them?"

I saw immediately what he was thinking. "Put the flyers in the cubbies?"

"Exactly." He turned and walked toward the office.

"But Mrs. Finch will be sitting there. She'll ask us what we're doing."

"I already thought about that," Tommy said. "Your job is to keep Mrs. Finch busy. Get her to come to the counter and talk to her while I sneak over to the teachers' boxes and put the flyers in."

"How am I supposed to do that?"

"I don't know. Talk to her about something," Tommy said. "Isn't your mom really good friends with her?"

"I guess. My mom works with the school parents' organization and sometimes Mrs. Finch helps out."

"Great. Talk to her about that. Just keep talking until I get all the papers in the slots."

"Okay," I said. The whole thing seemed kind of crazy, but also kind of exciting—like we were spies or secret agents. "What if she sees you?"

"Pretend you don't know me."

"But I *do* know you, and she *knows* I know you."

"Don't worry," Tommy told me. "Just keep her distracted."

"Okay, okay. But be fast."

"Fast is my middle name," Tommy said.

"Your middle name is Nelson," I said.

Tommy hung back, and I went up to the office counter. Mrs. Finch was at her desk, looking at some papers.

"Hi, Mrs. Finch," I said.

She looked up at me and smiled a big smile. "Oh, hi, Charlie," she said. "How are you?"

"Um, okay." I had to think of something to say. "But...but...I think I got a splinter from something and I wondered if you could just look at it."

She got up from the desk and came over to the counter. I saw Tommy slip behind her and hurry over to the teachers' boxes.

"Did you go by to see Mrs. Veazie?" she asked me.

"Who?"

"Mrs. Veazie, our school nurse."

"Oh right. *That* Mrs. Veazie," I said. "Um, no, I didn't see her in her office."

Which was true. I didn't see her because I didn't look for her.

"Let me see," she said.

"See what?"

"The splinter. Where is it?"

Boogers. What was I going to show her?

I stuck out the index finger on my right hand. "It really hurts," I said.

She took my finger in her hand and peered at it. "I don't see anything, Charlie," she said. "Why don't you just wait a little while and see if it gets better. If it keeps bothering you, then you should go see Mrs. Veazie."

"Okay," I said. "Do you know where she might be?"

I wished Tommy would go faster. I was having trouble thinking of something to keep Mrs. Finch from going back to her desk.

"She might be in the teachers' room eating lunch," she said. "You can look there."

She started to turn around. Tommy was still stuffing flyers in the cubbies.

He was going to get caught!

"Mrs. Finch!" I yelled.

"What?" She turned back, frowning. "Does it really hurt that much?"

"No! I mean, kind of, but I was just going to ask you…I mean…my mom, um, my mom wanted me to ask you if there was anything she needed to do."

"About what?" she asked.

"I can't remember exactly," I said. "Maybe about the next parents' meeting? Or something…"

Tommy was still stuffing papers into boxes.

Mrs. Finch folded her arms. "No, Charlie, nothing I can think of."

"Oh, okay," I said, "because sometimes she gets a little mixed up about things, so…"

I could tell by the look on her face that she wasn't believing anything I said.

I wouldn't have either.

She came around from behind the counter and looked down at me. "Charlie," she said, giving me a squinty, suspicious eye. "Aren't you supposed to be somewhere else? It seems to me like you're just wasting time here."

"Um, yeah," I said. "I mean, not wasting time. But it's my lunch period."

"Have you already eaten?"

Tommy was putting the last papers in the slots. Almost done!

"No." I held up my lunch bag so she could see. "I, uh, thought I would come here first."

"Why don't you go back to the cafeteria, have your lunch, and then see if your finger still hurts. When you get home, tell your mom there's nothing she needs to do about the parents' meeting."

This time when I looked behind Mrs. Finch, Tommy was down on his hands and knees, crawling behind her desk, headed for freedom. Mrs. Finch started to turn toward her desk. She was going to see him!

Eeek! What else could I do?

I hugged her!

"Thank you so much, Mrs. Finch," I said, my head buried in her armpit. "It's really been great talking with you."

"It's nice to see you, too, Charlie. Go back to the lunchroom."

Tommy was out of the office. My heart was thumping like a big bass drum.

I walked out as casually as I could and headed back to where Tommy was waiting.

"The cafeteria is the other way, Charlie," called Mrs. Finch.

"Right. I guess I forgot."

I turned back toward the lunchroom. When I was past the office, Tommy caught up with me.

"Stupific," he said. "Mission accomplished. No sweat."

"I can't believe I hugged Mrs. Finch. Never again."

"Never say never," he said. "It was a brilliant move."

I had to admit, even though I'd almost had a heart attack and Mrs. Finch thought I was weird, it really felt like things were going great.

Until we got to the lunchroom.

12

What Are Jerzollies?

Tommy got in the cafeteria line. I had my lunch bag, so I went right to our table. Hector was sitting with Trevor David and Maurice D'Aulaire.

"Where were you?" Hector asked.

"I had to go talk to Mrs. Finch." I sat down and opened up my lunch bag.

Turkey sandwich. Cheese and mustard. No lettuce. My dad was an expert at making my favorite sandwich. Plus, he gave me potato chips, which my mom will not put in because she's a health nut and she says they're fattening. But since Dad is working at home now, he's in charge of lunches and he always buys the little bags of chips.

Which I love.

I started to take out my sandwich and then I heard someone behind me.

"Hey, Charlie. Hey, Hector."

It was Darren. Standing beside him were Jaden and Butler.

I looked at Hector. The color had gone out of his face.

"Hi, Darren," I said. I was nervous, too.

"Hey, Hector," Jaden said, ignoring me. "Are you going to eat those cookies?"

I looked at Hector's tray. Two cookies were sitting there.

I knew Hector—he was very methodical about everything and ate one thing at a time. He was saving his cookies for last.

"Didn't you guys get some?" I asked.

"Not enough," Jaden said. "If you're not gonna eat them, Hector, it would be really nice of you to let me have them."

"I don't know," Hector said.

"Well, if he's not sure, I guess it's okay then, right, Jaden?" Butler said.

Hector shrugged.

"Great." Jaden started to reach for the cookies.

"Hector didn't say yes," I said. My voice was completely wimpy—I didn't sound very threatening.

"He didn't say no, either." Jaden grabbed Hector's cookies, stuffed one in his mouth, and broke the other one in half for Darren and Butler.

Trevor and Maurice just sat there with frightened looks on their faces.

"Hey, Charlie," Darren said. "I love that kind of potato chips. Can I have one?"

"No, Darren," I said. "It's just a small bag and—"

Just then Tommy showed up and plopped his tray down on the table. "I'm starving," he said without realizing what was going on.

"So am I," Darren said, snatching the bag of chips out of my hand.

"Hey!" I said.

"Just a couple," he said. Jaden started to laugh

79

while Darren opened the bag and stuck in his hand. Trevor was looking around for Mrs. Garrett, the new lunchroom monitor on that day. Darren pulled out a big handful of potato chips, and the rest spilled on the floor.

"Hey!" Tommy said. "Cut it out! Those are Charlie's chips!"

"Not anymore," Darren said, cramming them in his mouth. "He said I could have a couple." Chip crumbs sprayed out of his mouth as he talked.

"And by the way," Jaden said, "thanks." He reached out and swiped the cookies from Tommy's tray. Then the three of them turned and walked away.

"You bozos!" Tommy yelled. "You jerks! You, you, you…Jerzollies of Darkness!"

Jaden and Darren and Butler turned around and looked at us like we were Crog and Trog, three-headed alien brothers from the planet Bronador. They laughed, spewing bits of cookies and chips everywhere, then walked out into the hall.

"What are Jerzollies?" Trevor asked when they were gone.

I looked at Hector. He was staring at the floor. I felt worse than ever.

"I hate those guys," Maurice said.

"Maybe we should tell Mrs. Garrett about what happened," Trevor suggested. Trevor always wanted to follow the rules. "What do you think, Charlie?"

Without saying anything, I got up and walked over to Mrs. Garrett and stood there waiting for her

to finish talking to a couple of girls from fifth grade. Finally, she stopped and looked at me. "Yes, what is it?"

I wasn't sure if she knew who I was. "Mrs. Garrett, I'm Charlie Bumpers. Some older kids are bugging us. They're taking food from us without permission. And they won't stop."

"Did you do something to make them mad?"

"What?" I didn't know what she was talking about. The kids took our food, and she was asking if *I* did something wrong?

"You kids are fighting over food all the time," she said, shaking her head. "Can't you solve this by yourselves?"

"We tried," I said. "But they didn't listen."

"Well, I'm sorry to hear that." She sounded annoyed. "Let me know if it happens again. But it would be better if you kids would just try and get along."

She glared at me like I was supposed to learn a lesson from everything she'd said.

I *had* learned a lesson. The lesson was she wasn't going to listen to me. I turned and headed toward our table—everybody watched as I walked back.

"What did she say?" Tommy asked.

"She told me we should solve the problem ourselves."

"Ridiculous," Tommy muttered.

Everybody shook their heads.

"How are we supposed to do that?" Maurice asked.

"I don't know," I said. "But I'm going to figure something out."

"Me, too," Tommy agreed.

"Those guys are big," Maurice said. "You guys are crazy."

We knew that already.

13

Superior Mental Powers

Tommy called me on the phone that night. "We have to conquer the Jerzollies," he said.

"Tommy, we can't conquer them. They're bigger than us. We'll get destroyed."

"No, not in a fight. We'll have to use superior mental powers."

"Oh," I said. I wasn't sure we had superior mental powers. "Like what?"

"I don't know. That's why I called you," Tommy confessed. "Maybe we make them look bad somehow? Or embarrass them."

"We'd have to do it anonymously," I said.

"Right!" Tommy said. "That way we would be safe."

"Yeah." I had an idea. Talking to Tommy always gave me ideas.

"Why don't we use the Secret of Advertising? We could make flyers that announce they're bullies. And jerks. And bozos. Jerzollies!"

"I'm not putting any more flyers in teachers' mailboxes," Tommy warned.

"And I am *not* giving Mrs. Finch another hug. We won't even have to go to the office. We'll just put these flyers where kids will see them."

"Okay!" Tommy said. It sounded like he was bouncing up and down on something. Maybe his bed. "And this time we'll do something better. Like posters on bigger paper!"

"Hey! If you do it tonight, you could print them on your dad's copier."

I heard him stop bouncing. "Um, I don't know," Tommy said. "My dad told me it was kind of a special thing to use his copier."

"Tommy, just ask him one more time. Be a Hero of Vengeance!"

"Hmmm. Okay," Tommy said. "My dad's got a meeting tonight. So maybe he just wouldn't notice."

"Stupific," I said. "You're a genius."

"Um, I think this might have been your idea," Tommy said.

"You called me," I reminded him.

"But you thought of the posters."

"But you're going to print them."

"Okay, both of us," he said.

"Both of us," I said.

"Heroes of Vengeance!" Tommy said in his sports announcer voice. "The Jerzollies' bullying days will be over!"

"Power to the Heroes of Vengeance!" I shouted back.

I hung up the phone. And saw Mom standing in the hallway.

"What was that about?" Mom asked.

"Um, nothing," I said.

"Nothing?" She fixed me with the evil eye of motherhood.

"Not really," I said.

"What were you saying about hugging Mrs. Finch? Is there something wrong?"

Oh no. EMERGENCY MODE! More interrogation!

"Um, I gave Mrs. Finch a hug because she helped me with my finger. But it's nothing. I thought I had a splinter in my hand. And I didn't, see?" I held out my finger.

My mom is a nurse. She is an expert splinter remover. And also an excellent splinter finder. She took my finger in her hand and looked at it.

"I don't see anything," she said.

"I know," I said. "I told you."

Mom gave me another one of her looks—the is-everything-okay? look, which is another part of Emergency Mode.

She put her hands on my shoulders. "Charlie, are you sure everything is okay?"

"Yes!" I said. "Mom, it's okay."

"I'm going to talk to Hector's mom and see how they're doing."

"Maybe you could tell them they should stay," I suggested.

"I'll tell them we'll miss them if they go. How's that?"

"It's not the same," I said.

After Mom stopped giving me her special Mom Looks, I went to my room, shut the door, and lay down on my bed. Things were getting more and more confusing.

I heard my door open.

"Get out!" I said, thinking it was the Squid, who loved coming into my room.

"Sorry, Charlie," Matt said. "No can do."

I sat up. My brother hardly ever came into my room. What did he want?

He picked up a tennis ball that was lying on the floor. He started throwing the ball against the wall and catching it when it bounced back.

"What was Mom giving you a lecture about?"

"I don't know," I said. I wasn't sure how to start.

"Yes, you do," he said, bouncing the ball against the wall. "And you have to tell me or I'll just keep bouncing this ball against your wall all night."

"I *can't* tell you," I said, thinking of my promise to Hector. I'd told Tommy, but that was different.

"You have to. I'm your older and wiser brother."

I gave up. Maybe I did need to tell someone. "Well, it's about Hector, and these guys who are bugging him."

"Who's bugging him?" he asked.

"Darren Thompson."

"That kid who pulled your underwear out of your pants?"

"Yeah, and this fifth grader, Jaden Craig."

"I remember him," Matt said. "He's really big, right?"

"Yeah. And there's another kid, Butler something."

"Ugh, no. Not *him*. He's a little punk."

Butler didn't look like a little punk to me. He looked like a *big* punk.

"They're bugging Hector and picking on him," I told Matt. "We don't know what to do."

Matt bounced the ball against the wall five or six more times without saying anything. I guess bouncing the ball was how he thought.

"What do you think we should do?" I asked.

Matt stretched, tossing the ball up in the air. "Charlie," he said, "one thing to keep in mind. There are some people you just have to avoid if you can."

"I know, but it's hard to do that all the time."

"Well, if Jaden and those guys get too weird, you'd better tell someone at school. And by 'someone,' I mean a grown-up."

"But I don't want grown-ups making a big deal out of it," I said. "And Hector really doesn't want us to."

Matt shrugged. "Sometimes you have to tell someone anyway."

He started to leave the room and then turned back. "And another thing," he added. "If you and Tommy are in charge of running the campaign for Hector, he'll never be chosen, because you two can't do anything right. Which is actually a good thing in this case, since, like I said, it's the Kiss of Death. But if you decide to go ahead with it, what you guys really need is a campaign manager."

"What's that?"

"It's someone smart to be in charge of Hector's campaign, not you two bozons."

"What's a bo-zon?"

"A boson is a subatomic particle. But applied to you and Tommy, it's a bozo and a moron put together—'bozon.'" He turned and started to leave. Then he whipped around and threw the ball at my head.

"Hey!" I shouted.

"Just keeping you on your toes, Charlie."

I could hear him laughing all the way down the hall to his room.

14

Bombardment!

"Look at these!" Tommy said, pulling a sheaf of papers out of his backpack. He held one up for me to see.

Jerks + Bozos + Bullies = Jerzollies
Jaden + Darren + Butler = the Jerzollies of Darkness

"Wow. These are amazing!"

"I know. I used my dad's copier again. But this is the absolute last time. I think he only let me do it because he didn't know I was doing it."

Now that I was looking at the poster, I was beginning to feel a little nervous. "We have to make sure those guys don't see us doing this," I told Tommy. "If they find out it's us, we'll never get out of school alive."

He nodded. "We'll only put them up when no one's around. It'll be a mystery, just like who's running the Hector for Ambassador campaign."

"We could probably put up a couple before school, if we can find a place where no one is walking around."

"I know the perfect place!" Tommy gushed. "The gym!"

"But what if General Shuler catches us? That might be worse than being caught by the Jerzollies of Darkness."

I'd already had problems with Mr. Shuler, our PE teacher. He always acted like the gym equipment belonged to him and he never let us use it, so we called him General Shuler, Supreme Intergalactic Commander of Soccer Balls.

"He's on bus duty in the mornings," Tommy reminded me. "It'll only take us thirty seconds to put up a couple of posters."

The bus pulled into the school circle and we all filed out, right by General Shuler, Supreme Intergalactic Commander of Soccer Balls.

Once we were past him, Tommy whispered, "The coast is clear. It's time for the Heroes of Vengeance to strike!"

"Oh, man," I said. It seemed a little crazy, but I did feel like we were some kind of superheroes, fighting the Jerzollies of Darkness.

◆ ◆ ◆

We pushed open the gym doors and let them close behind us.

"Let's put them right here on the doors," Tommy said. "That way people can't miss them."

Tommy handed me the stack of posters. I took one and held it up on the door while Tommy tried to get the roll of duct tape out of his pocket. Finally he pulled it loose, but he fumbled it and it rolled across the gym floor.

"Hey!" we heard someone yell. "Look who's here!"

Before I could turn around, something hard hit me in the head. I fell against the door and slid to the ground, unsure of what was happening. I looked up at Tommy just as a basketball smacked him right in the stomach.

"Ooof!" he groaned and buckled over.

I twisted around to see where the balls had come from. Jaden and Butler were standing under the nearest backboard.

Before Tommy and I could get up, Jaden reached over into a metal cage and picked up another basketball. "Let's get 'em!" He grabbed another ball and tossed it to Butler. "Let's play Bombardment!"

My dad had told me about Bombardment. It's a dodgeball game kids play with volleyballs, picking teams and trying to hit the people on the other team with balls. He said they used to play it in gym class when he was a kid, but the coaches stopped it because kids kept getting hit in the head.

They didn't let us play it in our gym either. Not even General Shuler wanted us to play Bombardment. Especially not with basketballs.

But we were playing it now.

And we were the kids getting hit in the head.

Butler and Jaden walked toward us, holding the balls up, ready to throw. I was trying to get up but still felt kind of woozy from the first hit. And scared.

Tommy scrambled to his feet and ran over to pick up one of the loose basketballs. Two balls flew straight toward him from Jaden and Butler's hands.

One hit him in the shoulder, and the other ricocheted off the wall and bounced right back to Butler.

"Stop it, you jerks!" Tommy screamed. "You stupid bozos!" He hurled his ball at Jaden, who caught it on a bounce and moved closer to us. By then I was on my feet, so I ran over to join Tommy in the corner.

Bad idea! Now we were trapped.

Butler grabbed two more basketballs out of the cage and ran at us.

Before I knew it, there were basketballs flying and banging all around us, some of them hitting us, some bouncing off the wall back to Jaden and Butler for them to throw again. We shielded our heads the best we could.

The Heroes of Vengeance were being destroyed by the Jerzollies of Darkness.

Another ball slammed into my side. Suddenly I was furious. I almost forgot how scared I was. I chased down the closest ball and held it up in front of me. "Stop it!" I screeched.

A ball came flying at my head. I held up the ball I was using to shield myself, but the other ball knocked it out of my hands. Another one hit me in the leg. Tommy was picking up balls and flinging them back as fast as he could, but Butler and Jaden kept coming closer and closer, throwing harder and harder. They had us pinned in the corner.

"AAAAAAAAH!" Tommy yelled like some weird space warrior, and charged Jaden and Butler, holding the ball in front of his face.

Jaden and Butler only laughed and ran around the gym, turning every once in a while to hurl a ball at Tommy.

I grabbed a loose ball and took off after them.

I was so furious that I couldn't see straight, but I threw the ball with all my might. I started picking up any ball near me and chucking it as hard as I could without even looking.

Just as Tommy bent over to pick up a ball, another one from Jaden hit him in the side and knocked him over. I wanted to help him, but Butler had me cornered again. I heaved the ball at him and by some miracle it hit him in the head.

That got *him* mad.

"Now you're dead!" he shouted, taking a step closer to me. He was holding up the ball, ready to throw it.

"HEY!" an adult voice roared.

No one listened.

Butler threw the ball and it missed me. It bounced off the wall and I caught it.

"Bumpers! Stop it!" the voice called again.

I turned around.

It was the Supreme Intergalactic Commander of Soccer Balls.

His scowling face was already as red as a glowing stoplight.

"What do you think you're doing with my gym equipment?" he yelled.

I guess he was Supreme Intergalactic Commander of Basketballs, too.

Everyone had stopped to look at him except for me. I was still furious. I threw the ball I was holding at Jaden. It missed, bounced across the gym, and rolled right toward General Shuler.

"I said, 'Cut it out!'" General Shuler bellowed, stopping the ball with his foot.

Then he kicked the ball. Hard. Really hard.

I'd never seen anyone kick a basketball that hard.

It flew back across the gym while we all stood there watching it.

It smacked against the other wall, making a noise ten times louder than Mrs. Burke's exploding fingers.

KABLAM!

It bounced toward me and I scooped it up.

"Get over here, all of you!" the Supreme Commander shouted.

We walked over toward Mr. Shuler. I held the ball up, ready to protect myself in case anyone hurled something at me.

"Give me that ball!" Mr. Shuler's voice echoed all around the gym.

I handed it to him.

"What do you guys think you're doing?"

My chest was heaving in and out. I was gasping to catch my breath and keep from crying. Tommy was panting like he'd just run a marathon. Jaden and Butler were smirking. I hoped General Shuler would see what had happened and they would really get in trouble.

"We were just playing a game," Jaden said.

"What?" Tommy and I both said at once. This wasn't a game! It was a massacre!

"Bombardment," Butler explained. "All of us were playing."

Tommy turned to Jaden. "You weren't playing a game! You *attacked* us!"

"You threw the balls at us, too," Jaden retorted.

"We had to," I said. "You were trying to kill us."

"Sor-ry," Butler said in a mocking voice. "We didn't mean to hurt you."

"That's not true!" Tommy said. "You *did* want to hurt us!"

"We thought you liked playing," Jaden said. "That's why we kept throwing."

"Liar!" Tommy shouted.

"Enough!" Mr. Shuler said. "You guys know I have rules in my gym."

"It wasn't our fault!" I yelled.

Mr. Shuler turned and looked down at me. "Don't point the finger at someone else, Mr. Bumpers," he growled.

103

"It's not fair," Tommy said.

"I said shut up!" Mr. Shuler yelled.

My breath caught. I had never heard a teacher tell someone to shut up.

It's good he didn't have my mom for a parent. He would have been sent to his room. Without his basketballs.

As soon as he said it, he realized he shouldn't have. He took a deep breath. "All right, gentlemen. Let's all calm down."

"We're really sorry, Mr. Shuler," Jaden said. "All of us are, right?" He looked at me and Tommy and nodded like we should all agree with him.

"But—" Tommy started.

"Enough! No more arguing," General Shuler interrupted. "You guys have no business being in here. Do you want me to talk to your teachers and Mrs. Rotelli about this?"

Jaden and Butler looked down at the ground and shook their heads. Tommy and I looked at each other and didn't say anything.

"Shake hands," Mr. Shuler ordered. "All around."

I was standing next to Jaden. He turned and held his hand out to me, smiling. Butler did the same to Tommy. Tommy put his hands in his pockets and glowered.

"Do it *now*," Mr. Shuler commanded.

Tommy and I stuck out our hands and shook with Jaden and Butler.

"I'm going to overlook this," Mr. Shuler said. "But I don't want to see you messing around with gym equipment again. Now get back to class." He pointed to the door at the far end of the gym, where the posters were spread on the floor. "And whoever made that mess over there, clean it up."

"It was Tommy and Charlie," Butler said, grinning. "They were putting something on the door."

"Like I said, whoever made the mess, clean it up." Mr. Shuler glared at Tommy and me.

"Nice game, guys," Jaden said. "See you later." He and Butler left through the doors where General Shuler had come in.

Tommy and I ran over and started picking up the sheets of paper. Then we walked down the hallway, headed toward our classes. We walked by our custodian Mr. Turchin's office. There was a big gray plastic garbage can near the door. We didn't say anything to each other—we just dumped our posters in it.

"So much for the Jerzollies of Darkness campaign," Tommy muttered.

15

You Can't See a Stomachache

By the time I got to class, Mrs. Burke had already started teaching. She was telling the class about creating a personal narrative, which means writing about stuff that happened to you.

"Charlie," she said, looking at her watch. "Where have you been?"

"I'm sorry," I said.

"Where were you?"

"I was in the gym, talking to Mr. Shuler," I answered.

"As soon as you get off the bus, I expect you to

come right to class and get ready for your morning work," she lectured.

"I know." Now even Mrs. Burke was mad at me!

I plopped down in my chair and scowled. Unfortunately, she saw that, too. She glared at me for another second and then went on with the lesson. I opened my backpack and started putting things in my desk.

That's when I noticed that Hector wasn't in his seat.

Where was he?

Mrs. Burke divided the class into groups and started explaining how to put a story together by using a memory. But I couldn't listen. Nothing made any sense to me anymore, and even if it did, I couldn't tell the story I needed to tell.

Then Mrs. Burke told the class a story about falling out of a sailboat when she was nine years old, but I still couldn't get Jaden and Butler off my mind.

"Now, look at this list I've written on the board

and see if it reminds you of anything," Mrs. Burke went on. "I'd like you to pick one memory and then write a paragraph about it. After everyone is finished, we'll share them within our groups. Okay, get to work."

On the list were things like "A time you got in trouble," "Learning something new," and "A long car trip." All I could think of was what had just happened to me.

Everybody opened their writing notebooks and started to work. As I pulled mine out of my desk, some Hector for Ambassador flyers fell out into my lap. I stared at them.

I was really worried about Hector. Maybe he was just out sick. But he'd never been sick before. I couldn't remember a single day when he'd stayed home from school.

Mrs. Burke was walking around the room, looking at what people were writing. I got up and went over to her.

"Mrs. Burke," I said.

"You should be at your desk working, Charlie," she said.

"I know," I said. "But where's Hector?"

"He's out today," she said. "His mother called and said he had a bad stomachache."

"Do you think he's all right?"

"I'm sure he's fine," she said. "Now get to work."

I sighed and headed back to my desk. But I didn't write. I thought.

Maybe Mrs. Burke is right. Maybe it really is a stomachache.

Or maybe it's something else.

When I don't want to go to school, I always say I have a stomachache, since you can have one without having a temperature (which my mom, a nurse, ALWAYS checks), and you can't see if someone has a stomachache, like you can if someone has a cold or is throwing up. Throwing up you can definitely see.

If Hector didn't want to come to school, he might have just told his mom he had a stomachache.

And if he didn't want to come to school, it might be because he was afraid of Darren and Jaden and Butler.

I remembered what the Squid said about how sometimes kids who are being bothered by bullies avoid them by pretending to be sick.

And Tommy and I couldn't protect Hector from the bullies. Because they were bullying us, too!

And why even bother telling grown-ups? They either don't believe us or don't see what's going on.

"Charlie!" Mrs. Burke called. She was back at her desk. "Come here for a minute, will you?"

I got up and walked to the front of the room.

"Are you all right?" Her voice was a lot softer now.

"Yeah," I answered.

"Exactly what happened with Mr. Shuler?"

I couldn't decide how much to tell her. Part of me wanted to tell her everything, and part of me remembered that Hector had asked me not to talk about it. And another part of me was worried that if I told her what I thought really happened and she talked to Mr. Shuler, he would say I wasn't telling the truth, and then she wouldn't believe me anymore.

I wanted Mrs. Burke to believe me.

"Well, Tommy Kasten and I were in the gym before school started," I said.

"What were you doing in there?"

Trick question! No good answer! I didn't really want to tell her about the Jerzollies posters or the Hector for Ambassador Campaign. I wasn't sure she'd like either of them.

"We were just there for a second," I explained. "Then when we were leaving to come right to class these two kids started throwing basketballs at us and one hit me in the head so we started throwing balls back at them and then Mr. Shuler came in and told us to stop." I took a deep breath. "He got really mad."

I looked up at her. She was staring at my face like she could see inside my brain.

"Is that all?"

"Yes," I said.

"Who was throwing the balls at you?"

"Just some fifth graders that were in there." I was being careful because maybe Mrs. Burke would go into Emergency Mode, just like my parents, and I sure didn't want that. And I was still afraid of getting Jaden and Butler even madder at us.

She kept staring at me with her teacher eyes, searching for the truth. It was right on the tip of my tongue, but I just couldn't say it.

"Okay," she said, giving up. "You let me know if you need to tell me something."

"All right," I answered. My skin was prickly and I felt a little dizzy.

"Go work on your personal narrative."

I went back to my seat. Ellen Holmes, who sits in front of me, had turned around and was looking at the papers on my desk.

"What's this?" she said, holding up one of the Hector for Ambassador flyers.

I grabbed it and turned it facedown on my desk. "It's a secret campaign," I whispered.

"About what?"

POW!

Mrs. Burke's fingers exploded as she snapped them. Like a firecracker.

"Charlie, Ellen!" Mrs. Burke called to us. We looked up. She motioned for us to start writing.

Suddenly I had an idea. Ellen was really smart. And she had a bunch of friends. And she was really, really, *really* trustworthy.

"I'll tell you at lunch," I whispered.

"Okay." She smiled.

Ellen would make a great campaign manager. Why hadn't I thought of it before?

16

More Responsible Than the Heroes of Vengeance

Two hours later, Tommy and I were sitting at a lunch table surrounded by Ellen and two of her friends, Tara Billings and Tracy Hazlett. Being close to Tracy always makes me a little confused. I kept my eyes on Ellen so it wouldn't be so hard to talk. As I explained our secret campaign to get Hector chosen as School Ambassador, Ellen took notes.

I didn't know people ever took notes outside of class.

"So, here's your objective," she said, tapping her notebook with her pencil.

"What's an objective?" Tommy asked.

"What you want to accomplish."

Tommy nodded. "Right. Our objective."

"You want to spread the word that Hector should be School Ambassador, so that he'll stay here next year instead of going back to Chile."

"Right," I said. "We want the whole school to know."

"Kids aren't important for this," Tara said. "You need to convince the teachers."

Tara was in Ms. Lewis's class. She was a skinny, wiry, tough kid. I was pretty sure Darren had never bothered *her*. If he had, she probably would have slugged him.

"This isn't very good." Ellen held up a sketch Tommy had made for a new poster—it showed a dinosaur holding up a sign that said "Hector rocks!"

"Well, *I* like it," Tommy said.

"There's not enough information," Tracy said. "Why should Hector be Ambassador and not somebody else?"

"Because we want him to stay here next year,"
Tommy said. "Duh!"

Ellen shook her head. "That's not what I mean.
Why would Hector make a good Ambassador?"

"Because he would," Tommy said.

Ellen rolled her eyes. "No! You have to convince
the teachers. You have to give them good reasons
or they won't listen. 'Because he would' isn't even a
reason."

Tommy and I looked at each other and nodded.

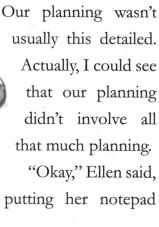

Our planning wasn't
usually this detailed.
Actually, I could see
that our planning
didn't involve all
that much planning.

"Okay," Ellen said,
putting her notepad

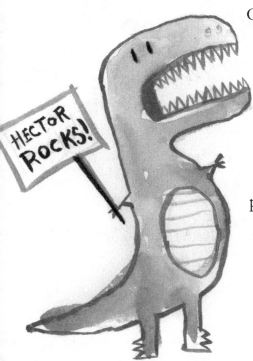

HECTOR ROCKS!

down on the table and getting ready to write. "Let's make a list of Hector's strong points."

"He's smart," I said. "Really smart."

"Good," Ellen said, jotting it down on the pad. "What else?"

"Responsible!" Tommy almost shouted. "Teachers love that word, and in this case, it's true. Hector is the most responsible kid I know. Like, he's much more responsible than—"

Tommy looked at me. I knew what he was thinking—he was thinking that Hector was more responsible than the Heroes of Vengeance.

I nodded.

"That's a good one, too," Ellen said as she kept writing. "What else?"

"He's really great at soccer," I said.

"Not important," Tara said.

"*I* think it is," Tommy said.

Tara glared at Tommy, like he should never challenge her. Tommy got quiet.

"Do you think Mrs. Rotelli and the teachers think being good at soccer is important for the Ambassador?" Ellen asked.

"Probably not," I admitted.

"Okay, then. What else?" Tracy asked.

I looked at Tommy. My brain was already fried from so much thinking. I could tell his was, too.

"Lots of stuff," Tommy said. "Like he can speak Spanish and English."

"Bilingual! Excellent." Ellen wrote that down. "Okay. One more thing."

I shook my head. I wouldn't have thought of all those strong points.

"I've got one more," Tracy said. "Hector is kind."

"Perfect," Ellen said, writing on the pad. "So here's our campaign slogan."

Hector Adélia—
Smart. Responsible. Bilingual. Kind.

"And stupific," I said.

"What kind of word is that?" Tara asked.

"A great word that means stupendous and terrific at the same time," Tommy said.

"Stupific. That's weird," Tara said. And when she said it, it did seem sort of weird.

"Okay," Ellen said, ripping the sheet out of her notebook and handing it to Tommy. "You make a poster with these words on it. Be sure and make the font really big, so people can read the words from a distance. And no dinosaurs this time. Can you get three hundred made by tomorrow?"

"Three hundred?" Tommy gulped. "That's a lot."

"That's what we need," Tara said. "Can you do it or not?"

"I guess so," Tommy mumbled.

"Stupific," Ellen said. "Bring them to me in the morning, and we'll get to work."

17

We Are So Dead

"Wow, there sure are a lot of buttons," I said to Tommy. I was staring at the huge copier in his dad's home office. Tommy had invited me over to work on the campaign poster while his dad was away. We had finished the document and printed it out. Now we were ready to make three hundred copies.

"I don't really know what all of those buttons do," Tommy admitted. "I just know you punch in how many copies you want and push the green one. When we finish this job, though, that's it. I'm definitely not printing anything else on my dad's machine."

"Does your mom know about this?" I asked. His mom was in the backyard with his sister Carla, working in the garden.

"Not exactly," Tommy said. "But this will only take a couple of minutes. It spits out the copies really fast."

"Where do we put the paper in?" I took the big package of paper I'd borrowed from my dad's desk out of my backpack.

"We'll figure that out when the paper in the machine is gone," Tommy said.

He lifted the lid of the copier and laid the poster facedown on the glass, then he shut the lid. When he pushed the copy button, lights came on, things moved around, and one flyer came out. Then it stopped.

"Do you have to print them one at a time?" I asked.

"No," Tommy said. "I forgot to push the button that says how many you want."

"Ellen said we should make three hundred," I reminded him.

"I'll push three hundred twenty-five. If we run out, we'll load in more paper."

Tommy pushed some more buttons. The machine beeped and whirred and clicked. Lights flashed, and then copies of the poster came rolling out of the copier, one after another. Every one of them told people to vote for Hector!

Then something clanked and buzzed and the papers stopped coming out. This time a red light flashed on and off.

"Something's wrong," I said. A little diagram appeared in the window near the buttons.

Tommy peered at the picture and screwed up his mouth. "I think it's jammed."

"That happened to me once when I was helping Mrs. Finch," I said. "I think we have to open up the machine."

Tommy started pushing buttons on the side of

the machine. Suddenly the whole top of the copier flipped up, and it seemed like we were looking at the insides of a car engine. It was so big I practically could have crawled in it.

"Wow," Tommy said, "look at all the parts."

"There's the paper," I said, pointing deep in the machine. "It's all sideways. See if you can just pull it out."

Tommy reached in and got hold of the paper. The printer made a cranking sound as he pulled on it. After he yanked the paper out, he closed the machine and pushed the start button. It printed ten or fifteen more copies, then clanked off again.

"Darn," he said. "Another jam."

We had to stop and open the machine three or four more times to unjam it. I was beginning to feel a little nervous. What if Tommy's mom came in?

The printer spit out a few more copies, then stopped. No flashing lights or clanks this time.

"What's wrong now?" Tommy said. "Stupid machine!" he yelled at it.

"It says here that it's out of paper."

"At least it's not another jam," Tommy said. He opened the paper drawer and I put all of my dad's paper in it.

We closed the drawer, lowered the lid, and pushed the green button. It was quiet for a moment, then it started to print again.

"Hurry up, hurry up," Tommy said, talking to the copier like it was a human.

The papers were flying out of the copier now. I looked at one as it came out.

"Tommy, look," I said. "The words are getting fainter. Like it's running out of ink or something."

"Argggh!" Tommy pushed another button and the machine stopped.

Now I was really feeling panicky and I could tell Tommy was, too.

He opened the machine. "Where's the ink thing?"

"I think this is it." I reached in and unhooked a long black plastic tube. It was sealed and snapped tight on the ends, but I managed to pry off one side and look in.

A little cloud of fine black dust rose up out of the tube when I shook it.

"It seems like it's full," I said.

"Let me see." Tommy took the cartridge from me. I looked down at my hands. They were covered with black powder. Tommy's were, too.

"Let's try it again," Tommy said. He snapped the cartridge back together and slipped it back in place, closed the lid, and pushed the green button again. There was black ink powder on the buttons of the printer, but it still worked. The machine whirred and clicked and started to print.

I grabbed the first copy that came out. "Look!" I said. "It's perfect! Except for the smudges from my fingers. This stuff is getting all over everything."

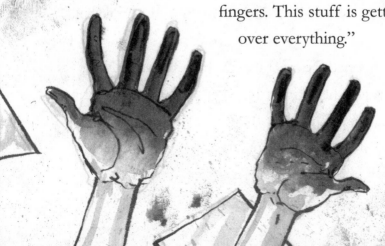

"There! Fixed it!" Tommy said. "We're geniuses. Now we just have to wait until it finishes."

We heard a door open. We both froze.

"Tommy!" his mom called from the kitchen. "I need some help out here." The door slammed again.

"Come on," Tommy said. "If you help me, we can get the job done really fast and then hurry back." We watched as the copier churned out three or four more copies of Hector's campaign, then we headed out to the garden.

Tommy's mom was down on her knees weeding between rows of little green plants, and Carla was digging in the dirt with a stick.

"Here we are, Mom," Tommy said.

"Gather up all those weeds and put them back there in the corner of the yard, please."

We carried out the weeds as fast as we could. Before she could ask us to do anything else, we scooted back up the steps into the house.

I followed Tommy into the house and back into his dad's office. But before we got all the way in, Tommy stopped in the doorway. I couldn't see what he was looking at. But I heard beeping and whining noises coming from the machine. It didn't sound good.

"Uh-oh," Tommy said.

"What?"

Tommy stepped into the room, and I pushed in behind him.

Disastrophe.

Copier paper was flying out of the machine and there were sheets of it all over the floor. Hundreds of them. A dozen different lights on the machine were flashing on and off—red, yellow, green, and even blue. Some of the sheets on the floor were perfect. But some of them were blank. And a few were completely black.

Tommy rushed over to the machine and started pushing buttons—but everything kept beeping and the paper kept flying out of the machine.

Then it just stopped. All the lights on it went out. No more buzzing. No more whirring. No more clanking. Just a dead copier.

Tommy opened up the machine and we looked inside.

There was powdery black printer ink everywhere.

Tommy started making strangling sounds. Or maybe it was me. Then we were both making strangling sounds.

And that's when Carla came in the room.

She took one look at us and the machine and the black splotches and the pieces of paper lying all over the room. Then she turned and ran out the door.

"Don't tell Mom!" Tommy yelled.

"Mommy!" she screamed, running down the hall. "Mommy! Mommy! Mommy!"

"We are *so* dead," Tommy said.

18

The Word Is Spreading

"I think I've seen my dad madder, but I can't remember when," Tommy said on the school bus the next morning.

I already knew his mom wasn't happy, because she had told us so when she found us trying to clean up the mess. "I am *not* happy!" she'd shouted. Then she'd called my dad to come get me.

The good news for me was she didn't say anything about the copier disaster to my dad. Tommy might die, but I might survive.

"What about the copier?" I asked Tommy.

"Dad got it to work again. He said that if it had been broken he would have had to sell me to buy the new parts. I think he was serious."

"I don't think you're allowed to sell your kids," I said.

"Maybe not. But I have to clean out the basement this weekend."

"That's not bad," I said.

"And clean up the dog park again," he muttered. "*That* you can help me with."

Oh no! Tommy's father was head of the parks department and made us clean up the dog park after we ate all the soccer team's candy bars and then lost the money we'd collected.

"Okay," I said glumly.

"I'll never get this stuff off." He held out his hands. They were still stained with black printer ink powder. I looked at mine. They looked just as bad.

"Me neither," I said. "Mom asked what happened, and I said I couldn't remember. But at least we have around two hundred campaign posters, even if some of them are kind of messy." I reached into my backpack to pull out the grocery bag full of campaign posters. I'd gathered as many as I could before I was banished from Tommy's house.

I held up one of the posters so we could look at it.

Hector Adélia—
Smart
Responsible
Bilingual
Kind
The Perfect Ambassador
BECAUSE HE ROCKS!

"I love the last line," Tommy said.

"Me too," I said. "I'll give them to Ellen. She told me Tara will be in charge of distribution."

"Tara kind of scares me," Tommy said. "I hope she doesn't do anything crazy."

"Me, too," I said. "You're usually in charge of the crazy stuff."

"Me? You mean *you're* in charge of the crazy stuff."

"Okay, okay," I said. "Both of us are in charge of the crazy stuff."

◆ ◆ ◆

Hector was at his desk, doing his morning work. He looked up and smiled at me. "How are you, Charlie?" he asked.

"I'm fine," I said, smiling back at him. Inside my backpack were the posters that said how great Hector was. I wanted to tell him about them, but I also wanted to surprise him. If we could get Hector to stay for next year, it would be stupific.

I slipped the bag of posters to Ellen when she came in. She pulled out one and read it. She frowned when she saw the last line but didn't say anything. Before I knew what was happening, she'd gotten permission from Mrs. Burke to go to the library and disappeared down the hall with the posters.

Mrs. Burke trusted Ellen more than she trusted me.

When Ellen came back, she didn't have the posters.

I wondered what had happened to them. It wasn't long before I found out. Hector was surprised. And I was, too.

◆ ◆ ◆

When we went to the restrooms to wash our hands before lunch, I was the first one in the boys' room.

I stopped when I got inside the door. I squeaked like the Squid does when she gets excited or upset.

Our posters were plastered on every mirror!

I glanced over and saw Hector in the mirror. He had come in and was standing next to me.

"Did you do this, Charlie?"

"No!" I said, which was true. "I just—"

Before I could say anything else, another group of boys came in. When they saw the posters on the mirrors, they started laughing.

"Hector! Hector! Hector!" they chanted.

"Hey, Charlie," Sam Marchand said. "How did you do this so fast?"

"I didn't!" I moaned.

"Boys!" a voice called from outside the restroom.

POW! The sound of exploding fingers. Mrs. Burke!

"It's time to come out now!" she called.

We all filed out. Hector was in front of me. His ears were bright red. He was walking and shaking his head and wiping his glasses all at the same time.

"Go line up in the classroom," Mrs. Burke ordered, her arms folded across her chest. As I passed her, I noticed one of Hector's campaign posters rolled up under her arm.

"I know about you, Charlie Bumpers," she said when I went by.

She knew! This was supposed to be a secret campaign! Now Mrs. Burke knew!

When we got back to class, the girls were already lined up at the door to go to lunch. I stood in line next to Ellen.

"What are you doing?" I asked. "Are you crazy?"

"Shhh!" she whispered. "The word is spreading."

"I know!" I whispered back. "Mrs. Burke thinks it's me."

"It *is* you! It was *your* idea!"

"Not to spread them all over the school! I just wanted to convince the teachers!"

"Change of strategy," Ellen said.

"They were even in the boys' bathroom."

"I know," she said, an evil smile on her face.

"Did *you* go in there?" I stared at Ellen with my eyes bugging out.

"Someone did," she said.

"I bet it was Tara," I said. "She's out of control!"

POW! More exploding fingers.

I looked up and Mrs. Burke was staring right at me.

After lunch, Mrs. Burke led us out to the playground. Everywhere I looked, I saw girls holding posters. I saw Tracy Hazlett hand one to Ms. Lewis, who tucked the paper under her arm and gave Tracy a hug.

I thought this was a secret campaign!

WHAT WERE THESE GIRLS DOING?

It got worse. Someone had given Alex McLeod, the most hyper kid in our class, a bunch of posters, and he was running around the playground with his crazy legs, handing them out to any kid he could find.

I avoided all the teachers until recess was over. I didn't want to have to explain.

"Holy moly!" Tommy said as we headed back into the school. "They even put a poster on the front door of the school!"

BOYS

19

Down in My Underwear

At the end of the day, as we walked down the hallway to our buses, I kept seeing campaign posters stuck up along the walls and on the doors.

Tara ran up and stood right in front of me. "We need two hundred more posters tomorrow," she ordered.

"Uhhh…I don't know if Tommy can do that."

"Tell him to do it or else," she said, and then went on ahead.

I wondered what "or else" meant.

I headed up the walkway toward my bus, and suddenly Jaden and Darren were on either side of me with Butler right behind. Each of them was holding a handful of campaign posters.

"Hey, Charlie," Darren said. "Cool poster."

"Uh, thanks."

"We found these on the floor in the hallway and we thought you'd want them back. We have an idea about where to put them."

"What? Um…where?"

"We'll show you," Jaden said.

Before I knew it, Butler had grabbed ahold of the back of my pants.

Oh no! I thought. *They're going to give me another wedgie!*

"No!" I yelled.

They didn't give me a wedgie. They just crumpled up the campaign posters and stuffed them down in my underwear.

Campaign posters inside your underwear are very scratchy.

They all laughed and headed for their bus. I watched them climb the bus stairs and sit down. Right behind Hector.

I pulled the wadded-up paper out of my pants and climbed on my bus. The Squid was sitting in one of the front seats with Carla, Tommy's sister.

"Charlie!" the Squid said, loud enough for everyone to hear. "What were those boys doing to you?"

"Nothing," I muttered.

"They were doing something," she said. "And I could tell they weren't being nice."

"Just forget it," I said.

"Were they being bullies?" she asked.

"No!" I said.

"If they were being bullies you've got to…"

Oh no. Not now. Not here!

The Squid and Carla got up out of their seats and started stomping their feet on the bus floor. "Stand up!" they sang out.

"STAND UP! And just say NO!

JUST SAY NO!

Until you make the bully GO!"

I ducked my head and lurched down the aisle to where Tommy was waiting for me. I plopped down in the seat, holding the crumpled campaign posters in my hands.

"What happened?" Tommy asked.

"Disastrophe," I said. "Campaign posters don't feel very good inside your underwear."

"I never would've thought to put posters down your pants," Tommy observed. "Nobody can see them there."

"Ha ha," I said.

When the Squid and I got off the bus, I said to her, "Hey, Squid, I need to talk to you about something."

"What?" she asked.

"You have to promise that you won't say anything to anyone about what you saw."

It was always tricky to get the Squid to do something—or *not* do something. She has a mind of her own, and it's a dangerous one.

Her eyebrows furrowed. "If someone's being bullied, you shouldn't keep it a secret. And not saying anything about what you saw is *almost* like keeping a secret."

"I told you, that wasn't me being bullied."

"Then what was it?" she asked.

"I don't know! It was me being teased. Those guys are just bozos."

"Isn't teasing like bullying?"

"Maybe sometimes. But it's not as bad."

"Teasing can be mean, though."

"Yeah, I guess," I said. "But this time it's okay."

"Still, teasing is almost bullying and if you don't stop the teasing, it will just turn into bullying, so I think you should tell."

"Mabel, just let me handle it, okay?"

"Okay," she said.

"Thanks," I said.

"Unless it really is bullying, then I'll have to—"

"No!"

"STAND UP! And just…"

Boogers.

20

Surrounded!

I reminded the Squid right before dinner to keep quiet about what happened. My sister has a very annoying way of saying exactly the wrong thing at exactly the wrong time, especially when it comes to something I've done.

She didn't mention it specifically during dinner, but she did bring up the subject of bullies.

"Mrs. Diaz says you should tell them how it feels when they bully you." She was holding up a green bean and pointing it at us while she talked. "We practiced saying it to each other in class. My partner was Carlos, and I told him, 'I don't like it when you tease me. It feels bad and I want you to stop it.'"

"Aha! So Carlos was teasing you?" Matt asked with a sly grin on his face. He was teasing the Squid, but she didn't notice.

"No, silly," the Squid said, waving the green bean at him like she was conducting an orchestra. "*I* was practicing asking him *not* to tease me. Someone had to be teasing me so I could practice telling them to stop. So I acted like he was teasing me so I could tell him to stop teasing me, and he acted like I was telling him to not tease me, even though he was only pretending that he'd teased me."

The Squid popped the green bean in her mouth, chewed for a few seconds, then swallowed it. She wasn't talking about what happened to me. But she sure was getting close.

Luckily, no one looked at me, and we finished dinner with no disastrophes.

After dinner, it was my turn to help Mom clean up.

"Honey," she said as soon as we had cleared the table, "I talked to Mrs. Adélia today."

I started putting the plates in the dishwasher. "What did she say?"

"She said they were going to leave sometime before the end of June. Hector will start school in Chile in July."

"He'll have to go to school in the summer? That really stinks."

"It will be winter in Chile. Their summer break isn't until December."

"Well, did you ask his mom if they *have* to move back? Why can't they stay just one more year? Hector is doing really well in school here."

My mom frowned at me and shook her head. "Charlie, his parents have important jobs. His father's company wants him back and his mom is going to teach at a college there."

"Yeah, but Hector has important things here, too."

"What do you mean?"

"Um...well, I think our school really needs him. Even the teachers want him to stay."

"I'm sure they do. I bet all the fifth-grade teachers would love to have him in their class."

"Even more than that!" I blurted out. "I think he's going to be a School Ambassador."

"They chose him to be School Ambassador?"

"I think they're going to. You can't say anything about it yet, though," I added.

She stopped scrubbing the pot in her hands and looked right at me. "If it's a secret, how do *you* know about it?"

Uh-oh.

"I don't know exactly. I just heard some people talking."

"Who?"

"Nobody," I mumbled. "Just forget it." I turned to leave the kitchen. Talking to Mom had gotten me all confused, and I didn't want to think about it anymore.

"Charlie, wait," Mom called. "I think you need to accept that Hector is leaving. I talked with his mom about having a big party before they go. It will be a nice way to say good-bye."

"Okay," I said. Although I didn't mean it.

"Do you understand?"

"Yes," I said. But I didn't. I was still hoping that Hector would be Ambassador, and then all the grown-ups who made plans without asking kids what they wanted would have to change their minds and listen for once.

Just this once.

When Tommy and I walked in the school the next morning, Mrs. Rotelli was standing by the front door.

"Hello, Charlie," she said. "Hello, Tommy." She had a Hector for Ambassador campaign poster in her hand.

"Hi," we both said.

"Can I see you boys for a minute?"

"Okay," we both said.

Boogers.

She led us over to the office but stopped before we got inside. "Mr. Turchin had a busy afternoon yesterday taking down all of these posters."

"We didn't put them up!" Tommy protested. "Somebody else did it. Not us!"

"Was it your idea?" Somehow Mrs. Rotelli managed to stare at both of us at the same time. Maybe that's how you get to be principal—you learn how to look at two kids at once.

"Well, yeah, kind of," Tommy admitted.

"It was our idea," I said. "But it was supposed to be a secret, and then it kind of got bigger than we thought it would."

"I see," she said. "And I suppose you were the ones who put the flyers in the teachers' mailboxes without permission?"

"Kind of," Tommy admitted.

Mrs. Rotelli stood there looking at both of us like we were Crog and Trog. I looked at the floor. Tommy looked up at the ceiling. Finally she said, "I understand you like Hector, and he may or may not make a good Ambassador. But it's the teachers' decision about who will be Ambassador next year, and they don't really need or want your help."

"Okay," Tommy said.

"All right, boys," she said. "You can return to class. And the next time you see Mr. Turchin you might want to apologize for giving him more work to do." She turned to leave.

"We just wanted Hector to stay!" I called out.

She turned back. "What?"

"Hector's parents want to move back to Chile this summer. And we thought if he was School Ambassador, they might decide to stay here."

Mrs. Rotelli's face softened. "Oh. Did Hector tell you that he and his family are leaving?"

"Yes, and we have to figure out a way to get him to stay."

"That's nice of you boys, but that decision is up to his parents, not you...or the teachers."

"Or Hector," I muttered under my breath. We headed back to class.

After lunch, we went out on the playground for recess. Tara and Tracy were standing by the fence with Tommy. I went over to join them and Ellen came up a few seconds later.

"Charlie, are you ready for the next step?" Tara asked.

"I don't know," I said. "What is it?"

"Tell them it's crazy, Charlie," Tommy pleaded. "I told them but they didn't listen."

"We're going to make a big banner to hang up in the hallway," Tara said.

"What? Where?"

"We haven't figured that out yet," Ellen said. "We were thinking over the gym doors. There's a big space there."

General Shuler's gym? BAD IDEA!

"I think maybe we've done enough campaigning," I said. "Mrs. Rotelli already knows it's us."

"It's only a couple more days," Tara said. "It's going to work!"

These girls were crazy.

I shook my head and turned away. As I did, I glanced over toward the Corner.

Oh no.

I didn't call out to Tommy or Ellen or Tracy or Tara. I just took off running toward the Corner. Like Buck Meson. Or Mercury. Or Charlie Bumpers.

To the rescue.

Hector was surrounded by the Jerzollies of Darkness.

21

The Weirdest Thing Happened

Jaden, Darren, and Butler had Hector cornered. He was holding his glasses in one hand. As I headed toward them, I saw Jaden push Hector in the chest.

My heart pounded, and I could hear myself panting. Not because I had been running. Because I was scared. And angry. And determined.

I had to stop it.

"Hey!" I shouted.

They all turned and looked at me.

I ran up and stood next to Hector. Now we were *all* in the Corner, out of sight of the teachers and most of the kids on the playground.

"What are you doing?" I asked. Really, I knew what they were doing, but it was all I could think of to say.

"Get out of here, Charlie," Butler warned.

"You guys need to stop bothering Hector!" *I must be crazy*, I thought. My heart was leaping up in my throat.

"Says who?" Jaden said, and took a step closer to me.

"It's okay, Charlie," Hector said.

I was sweating now. "No, it's not. Leave him alone."

"He doesn't mind," Jaden said. "And neither should you."

I wanted to be like Buck Meson. I wished I had an electron stare. I wished I could say, "I DON'T THINK SO" and zap him with a paralyzing ray.

"Just stop it," I said.

Darren wasn't saying anything—Jaden was the one doing all the talking, and Butler just had a sick smile on his face, like he was enjoying himself.

"And like *you're* going to make us stop?" Jaden said.

"Yeah." My voice sounded so weak. I wanted to speak up really loud and strong, but all I could get out was a lame croak.

"Oh sure," Butler said.

"Just leave him alone," I said. Then I looked past him at Darren. "Make them stop, Darren."

Darren put his hands in his pockets and looked down at the ground. I saw he was afraid, too.

"Okay," Jaden said, "we won't bug Hector. We'll bug someone else."

Before I knew it Jaden had shoved me in the chest with both hands. I fell backward over Butler, who had knelt behind me. I landed on my back and my head hit the ground.

Butler stood up and wiped his hands.

"Now, Hector," Jaden said, and took a step toward him.

There I was, lying on my back, looking up at Jaden and Butler and Darren and Hector. And the weirdest thing happened.

I thought of that dumb song that the Squid had been singing over and over.

"STAND UP!
And just say NO!
JUST SAY NO!
Until you make the bully GO!"

And so I stood back up. Hector was my friend, and it was time I stood up for him.

I stepped toward Jaden.

"You guys are bullies. Stop it."

Jaden shoved me again and there was Butler, right behind me again. I fell over him onto my shoulder.

I stood up again.

"Give it up, Charlie," Jaden said.

Jaden took another step in my direction.

"Stop it!" Hector said, and tried to grab him from behind, but Jaden shoved him away.

Jaden stepped toward me. I knew Butler was right behind me again, but I didn't care. I was just going to keep standing up until they got sick of knocking me down.

"That's enough, Jaden," Darren said. He was looking around like a mouse trapped in a cage, searching for some way to escape.

"No, it's not," Jaden said. And he pushed me again.

Oh man, I thought as I fell for the third time, *this could go on all day.*

And then out of the corner of my eye, I saw Tommy running toward us. Tara, Ellen, and Tracy were right behind him.

"Hey!" Tommy screamed. "Leave Charlie alone!"

I got up again and stood next to Hector. Butler and Jaden had turned to face Tommy and the girls.

I heard some yelling and then more kids came running around the corner. Joey Alvarez and Alex and Sam.

And even Samantha Grunsky!

Tommy and Tara reached us first.

Tara stood right up in front of Jaden, and I thought she was going to push *him* over. "You guys are big, stupid bullies!"

"Who are you?" he asked.

"We are the Heroes of Vengeance!" Tommy shouted before she could answer. "And we will defeat *you*, the Jerzollies of Darkness!"

That stopped everybody for a second. By then, a lot of other kids had arrived.

"Leave Hector alone!" Alex shouted. "We mean it!"

"Yeah," Joey said. "He's our next Ambassador!"

Suddenly, the Jerzollies of Darkness were feeling a little less sure of themselves. Butler and Jaden were still smirking, trying to act like they didn't care, but they seemed a little nervous. Darren sure didn't look like a bully anymore.

"Forget you guys." Jaden turned and gave me one more big push that sent me stumbling back against the wall.

"Stop it!" Tommy screeched, and jumped on Jaden. Tara jumped on him, too.

And then a whistle blew.

I knew that sound—I'd heard it a hundred times before. There was only one person who had a whistle like that.

The Ruler of Mrs. Burke's Empire.

22

Sometimes Exploding Fingers Aren't Loud Enough

Mrs. Burke wasn't running, but she sure was moving fast. Her face was about as grim as I'd ever seen it—her mouth was a straight line, and her eyes had fire shooting out of them. Forget the Buck Meson Electron Stare. Even an army of giant aliens wouldn't have a chance against the mighty stare of the Ruler of the Empire.

"What is going on here?" Mrs. Burke demanded.

Jaden turned to sneak away.

"Stop right there, Jaden," she said, standing in his path so he couldn't escape.

"These jerks were picking on Hector and Charlie," Tara said.

"They're bullies!" Joey shouted.

"One at a time," Mrs. Burke warned, holding up a hand. She turned back to Jaden. "What were you boys doing over here?"

"Um…we were just talking," Jaden said.

"It didn't look like you were 'just talking.' Pushing is not talking."

She paused, waiting for him to speak. But he just shrugged.

"Mrs. Burke," Alex piped up, "these guys were picking on Hector."

"And Charlie, too!" Tommy said. "I saw them push Charlie down."

Everyone started talking at once, pointing at Jaden and Butler and Darren.

Mrs. Burke blew her whistle again.

I guess sometimes even exploding fingers aren't loud enough.

"That's it," she said. "Everybody back to the playground. Charlie, Hector, Darren, Jaden, and Butler, let's go see Mrs. Rotelli."

"But Mrs. Burke," Darren whined. "I didn't do anything."

She gave Darren a long look. "Maybe that's the problem, Darren. You *should* have done something and you didn't."

Mrs. Burke led us across the playground, into the school, and down the hallway toward the office. I didn't really want to see Mrs. Rotelli again—she'd already lectured me once this morning. And every time we'd tried to explain ourselves, it hadn't gone very well.

"All of you sit here," Mrs. Burke said, pointing at the seats in front of the office desk. "Please keep an eye on these boys for a few minutes, Mrs. Finch." She rapped on Mrs. Rotelli's office door, walked inside, then closed the door behind her.

We sat and waited.

"Charlie," Darren whispered.

I looked up at him.

"What are you going to tell her?" he asked.

I shook my head. I didn't want to talk to Darren anymore. Ever. Again.

Finally, the door opened and Mrs. Rotelli was standing there with Mrs. Burke.

"Hector, could you and Charlie please come in here?"

I was nervous, but I felt this huge wave of relief roll over me. I had been afraid we were all going to have to go in there together and talk about what happened, and then Jaden, Butler, and Darren would gang up on me and convince Mrs. Rotelli nothing really happened, just like they had with Mr. Shuler. As I walked in, I decided I was tired of it. Hector was my friend, and I didn't like bullying. I didn't want Hector's memory of the end of the school year filled with those dumb Jerzollies. I wanted to stop them. Even if it meant talking to grown-ups.

Mrs. Rotelli told us to sit down. She pulled her desk chair around and sat right next to us.

"Boys, I'm going to ask you a question, and I'd like the truth. I need to know something and you are the only two who can tell me. Okay?"

We nodded.

"Were you being bullied?"

I looked at Hector. I was going to tell, but I wanted him to agree. He looked at the floor, then at me. Then he nodded.

"Yes," I said. "Jaden and Butler and Darren were bullying us."

"Is that right, Hector?" Mrs. Rotelli asked.

He nodded, then said, "They were mostly bullying me, and then they bullied Charlie because he tried to stop them."

"Okay," she said. "Now, I want you to tell me all about it. Just a minute." She went back to her desk, picked up her phone, and asked Mrs. Finch to get Ms. Colón, the school counselor. Then she came back over to us with a pen and notepad in her hand.

It was Emergency Mode.

But it was much bigger than at home—it was Supreme School Emergency Mode.

Ms. Colón came into the office, and then they both started to ask us questions. A lot of them.

They wanted to know everything—when the bullying started and how many times it happened.

I let Hector do most of the talking because it all started with him. I found out a lot of things that he hadn't told me. Those guys had been bothering him on their bus for weeks before I noticed anything was wrong. Hector said he couldn't tell anyone because his dad had always told him he needed to try to handle problems himself. His parents didn't know anything about it.

I told about the time I found Jaden cornering Hector in the boys' room and about all the times the three boys had taken other kids' food in the cafeteria and how we'd tried to stop it. Mrs. Rotelli wasn't happy when I told her that Mrs. Garrett told me to solve my own problems. When I described the Bombardment fight in the gym and told how Mr. Shuler had yelled at all of us, Mrs. Rotelli got a really annoyed look on her face and started writing furiously on her notepad.

Uh-oh, I thought. *What if she calls in Mr. Shuler?*

"I don't want to get in more trouble with Mr. Schuler," I said.

"You don't need to worry about Mr. Shuler," Mrs. Rotelli said.

Hector just sat there looking really worried. I knew what he was thinking.

"Do we have to tell our parents?" I asked.

"They need to know, Charlie," Mrs. Rotelli said. "I'm going to call them now. Do you understand?"

I nodded. So did Hector. "Okay," he said.

As we left the office, Mrs. Rotelli put her hand on my shoulder and held me back. "Charlie," she said, closing the door. I looked up at her.

"Thank you for standing up for Hector," she said. "I wish you had told us sooner so we could have helped you. No one should be bullied in this school."

"I wish I *had* told you," I said. "Am I in trouble?"

"No," she said. "But I'm afraid those boys waiting out there are." She gave my shoulder a squeeze.

And then she called in the Jerzollies of Darkness.

The classroom was really quiet when I came in. No one said anything, but everybody knew. At the end of the day, the Squid and I were called to the office. Mom was waiting for us there with Mrs. Rotelli. She had a worried look on her face.

"Why are you here, Mommy?" the Squid asked.

"Just needed to check on some things. Let's go."

On the way home in the car I was really glad Mom didn't tell Mabel anything. The Squid probably would have started singing that dumb song again, which was already stuck in my head for the rest of my life.

Dad was in the kitchen when we got home. "You okay?" he asked.

I nodded.

"Good. Go put your things in your room and come back down. Your mom and I want to have a talk with you." He had a serious look on his face.

Boogers. I was ready for all this to be over, but I knew Emergency Mode was going to go on and on for days. I headed up the stairs. Matt stuck his head out of his room.

"Charlie!" he said. "Get in here!" He stepped back and I walked in.

He shut the door with a quiet click.

"Okay, spill it. What did you do this time?"

"I didn't do anything! It's everybody else!"

"You must have done something. Mom and Dad are going nuts!"

I slumped down on his bed. "I don't want to talk about it."

"You have to," Matt said. "I'm the only person you can really trust."

That sounded completely ridiculous. But in a way he was right. Older brothers sometimes understand things that others don't. So I started to tell him and he listened.

"I told you to tell someone!" he finally said.

"I know!" I said.

"You should always listen to your older and smarter brother."

"I know," I said. "Except for the smarter part."

I still felt bad, but mostly I was relieved. It felt good to stop holding in the secret, and it felt good to know that the grown-ups were going to take care of the situation and I didn't have to worry about it. I was still nervous about seeing Darren and Jaden and Butler, though. And General Shuler, the Supreme Intergalactic Commander of Soccer Balls and Basketballs.

"Don't worry," Matt said. "Those guys won't bug you anymore."

"Good," I said.

"At least not until middle school," he added.

"Thanks, Matt."

"No problem," he said. Then he punched me in the arm, but not very hard, because he was just my moronic brother, not one of the Jerzollies of Darkness.

And then I had to talk with my parents—for a long time. It was definitely Emergency Mode, but by that time, I was almost used to it, and they weren't mad, just worried. Like I said, I just wanted it all to be over. I was glad they knew now and I didn't have to keep a secret anymore.

Some secrets you shouldn't keep.

By the next day, it seemed like the whole school knew what had happened. Darren, Jaden, and Butler weren't at school, and I stayed away from them when they came back. I didn't want to see them, and I guess they didn't want to see me. But I heard they got in big trouble.

Mostly, I hung out with my two best friends, Tommy and Hector.

The next time I went to gym class I wondered if Mr. Shuler would say anything to me.

He didn't. He acted like nothing had happened. In fact, he seemed to be avoiding me. I avoided him, too.

I hadn't forgotten Matt's words: "Charlie, one thing to keep in mind. There are some people you just avoid if you can."

I guess that's true for grown-ups, too.

23

The Kiss of Death

The end-of-year awards assembly happened a couple of days later, on Friday afternoon. First the chorus sang three songs, and then the first graders recited the King Phillip Elementary School Pledge.

And sang the bully song.

After Mrs. Rotelli gave a speech about what a good year this had been for our school and how proud she was of everyone, the teachers handed out awards in each grade to kids who had done service projects and done really well in writing contests and stuff like that.

I was looking around and kind of bored when

I saw Mom and Dad standing in the back of the room. What were they doing there? Maybe the Squid was going to win an award. I'd told them *I* wasn't going to win anything.

I sat there thinking about all the things I wouldn't win anything for.

I certainly wouldn't win anything for being wrapped up in toilet paper like a mummy.

Or falling off a desk trying to fix a picture.

Or throwing my shoe on the school roof.

Or being a really nice gnome and not an evil sorcerer.

Or writing a really dumb essay about what I'm thankful for.

Or losing our candy bar money on the bus.

Or having a messy desk.

Or dressing up like a rabid bat.

Or bragging too much about my dad.

Or knocking over twenty-five gallons of water

and a teacher in the hallway while I was running like Buck Meson.

Mrs. Rotelli called this year's School Ambassadors to the microphone. They each gave speeches about what it meant to them to go to King Phillip Elementary School and how the fourth graders were going to be fifth graders next year and how they would have to take care of everybody in the school.

I just wanted to find out if Hector was going to be Ambassador and stay here. That was all I really wanted.

When they finally finished, everybody applauded. Then Mrs. Rotelli went back to the center of the stage.

"Students and teachers, it is now my honor to introduce the two new Ambassadors for the coming year. These two students have distinguished themselves in their work and citizenship for the year. They will represent our school to visitors and on trips outside the school. Many are deserving, but these two are special."

I was thinking, *Hector! Hector! Hector! CHOOSE HECTOR! CHOOSE HECTOR!*

I looked at Hector, and he was paying really close attention. Maybe he was hoping like I was that he'd be chosen and would get to stay for another year.

"The first of the two School Ambassadors for the coming year is...Ellen Holmes!"

"What?" Ellen covered her mouth in surprise. The girls on each side of her tried to hug her at the same time.

"Ellen, please come up," Mrs. Rotelli said.

Awesome! I thought. Ellen would make a perfect Ambassador. And even if it turned out to be a crummy job, like Matt had said, she wouldn't mind.

As Ellen made her way to the front, I worried that they might not choose Hector, since then both Ambassadors would be from the same class. I hadn't thought about that.

"And," Mrs. Rotelli went on, "the second School Ambassador for next year is..."

She didn't say Hector's name.

At first that's all I realized. At least it didn't *sound* like Hector's name. People were clapping so loud, I couldn't think. But then Joey, who was sitting next to me, started pounding me on the back.

"Way to go, Charlie!" he hooted.

What?

Me?

That was impossible!

The Kiss of Death!

Mrs. Rotelli must have made a mistake!

"Charlie, please come up to join Ellen."

"I cannot believe this is happening," Samantha said as I walked by her.

I looked at my parents. Their smiles were as big as their heads. I walked by Mrs. Blumgarden, the fifth-grade teacher I had accidentally knocked over in the hall earlier in the year. She was applauding, too.

How could she have voted for me?

I walked up to Mrs. Rotelli.

People kept on clapping.

"Charlie! Charlie! It's me!" the Squid yelled. "You're my brother! Hey, everyone! I'm Charlie's sister!"

That was my sister, Mabel the Squid.

When I reached the front, Ellen gave me a fist bump.

I touched Mrs. Rotelli's sleeve.

"Yes, Charlie?" She leaned down so she could hear me.

"Mrs. Rotelli," I said, "I really wanted Hector to be School Ambassador."

She squeezed my shoulder. "I know you did, Charlie. I know you did." Then she held up her hand for quiet, and everybody stopped applauding.

"Ambassadors for our school must be good students," Mrs. Rotelli said. "But more important than that, they must be kind. They must be thoughtful and welcoming to others. Ellen and Charlie are all of those things and more. They will make great Ambassadors for the coming year."

Then everybody applauded again. And when I looked out into the audience, I could see that Hector and Tommy were clapping harder than anyone else.

Actually Tommy was whooping and jumping up and down in his seat. Until Mrs. L took him by the shoulders and gave him a squeeze. Just enough so he calmed down a little.

For once.

24

Saying Good-Bye

I guess the end of the school year comes, whether you want it to or not.

The last day of school was Tuesday, and it was only a half day. Instead of doing schoolwork, we spent the whole morning making a big list of the things we had done and learned in the past year. All the different kinds of math problems we'd learned how to do, all the books we'd read and liked, the field trips (including the visit to the colonial village, where Alex got stuck in the corn crib the sheep were eating out of), and a bunch of other funny things that had happened. And then we listed what we were going to remember most about our time in Mrs. Burke's Empire.

Every time we added another memory to the list, it reminded me of something about Hector, and it made me sadder and sadder. I couldn't believe he was leaving.

With only a little more time to go in the school day, Mrs. Burke asked us to face the front and pay attention. "A couple of people are leaving our school this summer," she said, "so I'd like for us to spend some time saying good-bye to them. Candy is moving with her family back to North Carolina. And Hector's family is moving back to Chile. If you'd like to say something to them, this would be a good time for all of us to hear it."

One by one, kids spoke about Candy and Hector. It was all really nice, but I started to get that faraway feeling I'd had when I first heard Hector was moving, or when I realized he was being bullied. Every time someone talked about Hector, it made me feel like no one really knew him as well as I did. Hector was one of my best friends. I felt so sad about him leaving that it was going to be hard for me to say anything at all. Finally, everybody else stopped talking and I saw Mrs. Burke looking at me.

"Anything to add, Charlie Bumpers, School Ambassador?" She gave me an extra serious look, like since I was School Ambassador I was expected to speak.

Maybe Matt was right. Being Ambassador *was* the Kiss of Death.

I forced myself to stand up.

"First," I said, "Candy was a great mouse in the play, and I hope she squeaks all the way to North Carolina." Everybody laughed.

"Then…" I took a deep breath. "I think we were all really lucky to have Hector in our class this year. I didn't know anything about Chile at the beginning of the year, and no one else did, either."

"I did," Samantha said.

I ignored Samantha and kept going. "We learned a lot that we wouldn't have known if he hadn't been here. He taught us a bunch of Spanish words, including what a *chupacabra* is. We also learned that you don't have to be loud or noisy to be a good friend. Hector was nice to everyone, right?"

Everybody nodded.

"Smart. Responsible. Bilingual. Kind!" Alex shouted.

POW! Mrs. Burke's exploding fingers. One last time!

"And don't forget," I went on. "He's a fantastic soccer player."

Sam Marchand and a few other kids cheered.

"So we were the lucky ones to…have…him for a year." I wanted to say *adios* to Hector, but instead I sat down quickly. I DID NOT WANT TO CRY.

Then Hector stood up. Which was surprising, because, like I've said many times, Hector is very quiet and sort of shy.

"I want to thank everyone for everything," he said in the accent I had grown so used to hearing. "*Gracias*, Mrs. Burke, for being such a good teacher.

And thanks to everyone in the class for making me feel welcome. And I especially want to thank Charlie, because he was the first one who became my friend and because he always helped me out when I was having a hard time. I won't ever forget Mrs. Burke's Empire. You should all come visit me in Chile. You can all be Ambassadors from Mrs. Burke's Empire!"

Everyone applauded and cheered. Mrs. Burke applauded and cheered right along with us.

When I looked more closely, I noticed something else.

The Ruler of Mrs. Burke's Empire had tears in her eyes.

25

And It Was Just Us

Tommy, Hector, and I were playing soccer in my driveway. I was the goalie, and my job was to keep the ball from hitting the garage door so Dad wouldn't yell at us. Everybody else—Tommy's family, Hector's parents, and my family—was in the backyard sitting around the picnic table.

Tommy, Hector, and I had decided there was no point in staying at the table, since there was no more pizza left.

I was concentrating on our soccer game, trying to forget what was about to happen. But then Hector's mom and dad showed up in the driveway, followed by everyone else.

"*Es tiempo, chico,*" Hector's dad said to him, pointing to his watch. "We don't want to miss the plane."

"What happens if you miss it?" Tommy asked hopefully.

"We take the next one," Hector's dad said, smiling.

"Boogers," I said.

Then Hector kicked the ball, and I was caught by surprise. It went right through my legs and banged really loudly against the door.

I grabbed it on the rebound and looked at Dad. He just smiled and shook his head.

I guess you don't get mad at someone when they're about to get on an airplane to move to Chile.

We all walked over to their rental car. Hector's parents gave hugs to the other grown-ups and kids. Then Hector's dad came over to me. "*Un abrazo, mi amigo*," he said. "Give me a hug."

I was surprised at that. But I gave him a hug. Then he held both of my arms, looked me right in the face, and said, "You, Charlie, are a good friend. You helped Hector when he needed it. And you will always be part of our family."

Wow. Mr. Adélia had never said much to me before. What could I say?

"Thanks," I said. Which is what you say, I guess.

"And thank you all so much for your kindness," Hector's mom said. "You've made us feel so welcome here."

"You're always welcome here," my mom said.

"Anytime," my dad said.

"And you are welcome in Santiago," Hector's mom replied. "Especially Charlie and Tommy."

"And me and Carla?" asked the Squid.

"Of course, Mabel," Hector's dad said. "All of you."

"You can call me the Squid," my sister announced. "I like it better. It's what Charlie calls me."

Everybody looked at her like she was the sister of Crog, the three-headed alien creature from the planet Bronador. The Squid smiled. She didn't care.

Hector's parents climbed in the car. Hector stood by the back door of the car, in a little triangle with Tommy and me. I was holding the soccer ball.

"Okay," Hector said. "I guess I have to go."

"How big is your suitcase?" Tommy asked. "Maybe we could hide inside."

Hector shook his head and grinned.

I didn't want Hector to go. Mom told me that maybe someday I could visit him in Chile. It was hard to believe that would ever happen, but maybe it would. I was never going to forget him.

"Here," I said, holding out my soccer ball. It was my favorite one—the spots on it were blue and green, and I had saved up my own money to get it.

Hector shook his head. "No. That's okay," he said. "I have a couple already. Thanks."

"You have to take it." I said. "It's a really good one."

"Thanks, Charlie," Hector said. "But you keep it."

"It's a really good one," Tommy said. "They might not have them in Chile."

"I want you to have it," I said. "It's the one you scored your last goal with in the United States. Against my garage."

He shook his head.

"And when I come to visit you," I said. "You can give me one of yours."

"Okay." He grinned. He took the ball. "Thanks."

I didn't know what to say then, because it was time for them to go.

Just then a car I didn't recognize pulled up to the

curb. Someone hopped out of the car and hurried toward our driveway.

Mrs. Burke!

It's weird seeing your teacher outside of school.

"Oh, good!" she said. "I'm not too late!"

Hector had a huge grin on his face.

"Are you sure you're not staying here?" Mrs. Burke asked.

Hector shook his head, smiled, and took off his glasses to clean them.

Mrs. Burke bent down and looked in the front seat.

"I came to say good-bye." She reached her hand in and shook hands with Hector's parents. Then she turned and held out her arms. "Give the Ruler of the Empire a big hug, Hector!"

And Hector did, which was surprising, since he's pretty shy. He was holding his glasses in one hand and my soccer ball in the other, so he couldn't squeeze very well, but he did his best. And she squeezed him back.

Hector's dad started the car and Hector climbed in. They backed out and pulled away. Tommy and I ran down the street, waving after them until the car turned at the corner and was gone.

And it was just us.

Mom and Dad.

And Matt.

And the Squid.

And Ginger.

And Tommy.

And Mrs. Burke.

And me, wondering what was going to happen next.

BILL HARLEY is the author of the award-winning middle reader novels *The Amazing Flight of Darius Frobisher* and *Night of the Spadefoot Toads*. He is also a storyteller, musician, and writer who has been writing and performing for kids and families for more than thirty years. Harley is the recipient of Parents' Choice and ALA awards, as well as two Grammy Awards. He lives in Massachusetts.

www.billharley.com

ADAM GUSTAVSON has illustrated many books for children, including *Lost and Found*, *The Blue House Dog*, *Snow Day!*, and *King of the Tightrope*. He lives in New Jersey.

www.adamgustavson.com

Don't miss the other books
in the Charlie Bumpers series—
Charlie Bumpers vs. the Teacher of the Year,
Charlie Bumpers vs. the Really Nice Gnome,
Charlie Bumpers vs. the Squeaking Skull,
Charlie Bumpers vs. the Perfect Little Turkey,
Charlie Bumpers vs. the Puny Pirates, and
Charlie Bumpers vs. His Big Blabby Mouth.

Also available as audio books.

HC: 978-1-56145-808-0
PB: 978-1-56145-888-2
CD: 978-1-56145-809-7

HC: 978-1-56145-732-8
PB: 978-1-56145-824-0
CD: 978-1-56145-770-0

HC: 978-1-56145-835-6
PB: 978-1-56145-963-6
CD: 978-1-56145-893-6

HC: 978-1-56145-740-3
PB: 978-1-56145-831-8
CD: 978-1-56145-788-5

HC: 978-1-56145-939-1
PB: 978-1-68263-001-3
CD: 978-1-56145-941-4

HC: 978-1-56145-940-7
PB: 978-1-68263-064-8
CD: 978-1-56145-942-1